HARLEY & HOMER

Oak Manor Publishing, Inc.

Manchester, New Hampshire

Designed and Published by

OAK MANOR PUBLISHING, INC.

Manchester, NH 03102

603-860-5551

www.oakmanorpublishing.com

Printed and bound in the United States of America

by Minuteman Press of Nashua

88 Main Street

Nashua, NH 03060

603-880-4890/Fax: 603-883-4893

info@nashuaminuteman.com

www.nashuaminuteman.com

Library of Congress Cataloging-in-Publication Data

Ciocca, Madonna S. 1951 -

Harley & Homer/Madonna S. Ciocca

p. cm.

ISBN 0-9747361-2-0   FIRST EDITION

COVER PHOTO Copyright © Mark Ciocca.

COVER DESIGN Copyright © Alex J. Schlesinger and John W. Greene

Oak Manor Publishing, Inc.

DEDICATION

It took a village to help write this book. I will begin with the beginning. My supportive writing group: Lenita, Jenn, Jackie, and Betty. My mother and father for always encouraging and supporting me. Cluster 7-1 students of Rundlett Middle School over a couple of years for helping me write for their age, especially to Lauren Greene, Carol and Mona, my childhood partners in crime. Sue, Mark, Bronwyn & Waters Funeral Home for helping with research. Liz Henley for proofreading. My three sons, Anthony, Andrew, and Abram, who have loved me through anything and everything.

Most importantly I acknowledge the one person without whom I would accomplish nothing. My husband, soulmate, and best friend Mark, who always makes sure that I am safe and warm and loved.

CONTENTS

HARLEY & HOMER

by Donna Ciocca

CHAPTER ONE

LIKE FATHER, LIKE SON

Harley and Homer were not the brightest bulbs in the chandelier. They were labeled "troublemakers" in first grade when Sister Germain had them both stand in the corner under the Saint Jude statue for time out. Saint Jude is the "Saint of the Impossible."

The boys just seemed to stick together like magnets. They were an odd pair, Homer was short and stocky and had red curly hair and freckles. Harley was tall and thin with brooding dark eyes and a small scar under his left ear. He wore his black hair long and straight, slicked back from his face. Even though they didn't share any physical traits they had a lot in common. Both of them hated school, both of them hated teachers and both of them hated their fathers. On the other hand, both of them liked hunting, eating pork rinds, motorcycles and getting into trouble (or at least that's what everybody in town believed).

Harley and Homer just couldn't stand to be bored, or the truth of the matter was things were not so great at home. If they ever found themselves with a little extra time on their hands they would start thinking and talking about what they could try. The problem, well at least one of the problems, was that the boys had little fear and less common sense. They would try anything, especially if it meant that they might gain something from it like money or food, or excitement, or fame and glory. They both *longed* for fame and glory. They wanted to be John Wayne, Clint Eastwood or any other macho movie star in the 1960s. Most often their schemes never turned out exactly as they planned.

Take, for example, the time they planned to prove that one of their teachers was a witch. They had just watched the Wizard of Oz and loved the part about a real witch melting. They were students in Sister Germain's fourth grade class. Sister Germain was one of those teachers who liked clean, quiet girls. She had no time or patience for two noisy boys who hated school to begin with. They couldn't even whisper without her getting all riled up. Her favorite line was "You two are going to end up in the penitentiary!" That line hurt Harley in particular because his dad was doing time in the "State Pen" and he was always telling Harley "Like father, like son!"

They called Sister Germain..."Sister Germ."

"I'm telling you that Sister Germ is a real witch!" Harley was discussing with Homer at lunch.

"Uh huh. Are you goin' ta eat the rest of that?" Homer pointed to Harley's mayonnaise sandwich.

"Dang it, Homer! Is that all you can think about is *my* food?"

"Well, I cain't think of my own 'cuz I already ate it!" He looked sadly at his empty lunch bag.

"Homer, we got to make plans to prove that Sister Germ is a real, honest ta God witch. That way they'll have ta git rid of her 'cuz it's against the Catholic religion ta have a witch be a member of the congregation." Harley handed Homer the last piece of his sandwich. He hated it when the meat ran out at home and the only thing left was bread and mayonnaise. But things could be worse, there were times when there was no bread either. On those days he would have to rely on Homer to share his lunch.

"How are we goin' ta get close enough to Sister Germ with a bucket of water so we can melt her? That woman has eyes in the back of her head. I hear tell that that is why nuns wear those veils. I also heard that they had operations on their eyes so's that they could see through things. She'd spot us comin' from any direction." Homer licked his fingers.

"We'll just have ta come up with somethin'. Don't we always?" Harley looked pleadingly at his partner.

"Yeah. All right. Have you got any ideas?" Homer knew

that Harley always had something cookin'.

"As a matter of fact I do. We only need an unsuspecting girl. Can you think of a girl that might help us out?"

"A girl! A girl ain't gonna help us out, Harley. They all hate our guts."

"Ah come on, Homer, there has ta be some girl that we could talk inta helpin' us. Maybe we could hire one."

"Well there might be one who kinda owes me a favor... but she's not quite a girl... she's Rhoda Lee Swampson." Homer wrinkled up his nose just at the thought of Rhoda Lee.

There's one like her in every class, a girl who doesn't like being a girl or maybe just doesn't know how. Rhoda Lee was number four out of seven children in the Swampson family. It seemed like the more kids the Swampsons had, the less they could take care of them. Rhoda Lee had always wanted to be partners in crime with Homer and Harley but they shunned her like the plague. They even nicknamed her "Rodent Lee."

"Now explain to me how a girl like Rodent Lee could come about owin' you a favor."

Harley knew this was goin' to be painful for Homer to tell 'cuz rumor had it that she had a crush on Homer like a Sumo Wrestler.

"Well do you remember when she had ta sell all of the candy bars for that church club she belongs to? She ate most of 'em and she came up short of cash."

"You stole money for Rhoda Lee Swampson?!" Harley interrupted.

"No! I did not exactly steal money for Rhoda Lee. I just kinda *borrowed* it."

"Nobody in their right mind would ever lend you any money, Homer! So what do you mean by '*kinda* borrowed' it?" Harley was gettin' loud.

Homer leaned in close and whispered, "I borrowed it from St. Joseph."

"Are you goin' loopy on me, Homer? How in the *hell* do you borrow money from a religious dead guy?" Harley yelled just as Sister Germain walked by their table.

"HARLEY!!! Did I hear what I think I heard?" She had her

arms folded and hidden in her billowy black sleeves.

"I don't know sister. You tell me what you think you heard and I'll tell ya if ya heard it." Harley looked up innocently and smiled.

"Or better yet, sister, why don't we just tell you what you heard so then you don't have ta think about whether you heard it or not?" Homer offered with a grin.

Just as Sister Germain was getting ready to lower the boom on the two friends, there was a screech from the table behind her. A lunch tray went flying off the table as Rhoda Lee Swampson yelled "Cockroach!!"

The nun jumped up onto the bench next to the table. Sister Germain had a phobia when it came to bugs. She was busy dodging weenies and beanies and invisible cockroaches so she didn't see Rhoda Lee wink at Homer.

"You may be onto something, Homer. Rodent Lee might be *just* the girl we need." Harley and Homer leaned in close once again to talk about the plan.

There were two boys' bathrooms in the school. In the newer addition the bathroom was more modern. The old original bathroom had fixtures that were older than dirt. It was the bathroom Harley and Homer hung out in, where they felt more at home.

The boys knew that they could find a bucket in that bathroom because it had been there under a sink collecting the water from a small leak in the pipe for two years, since the boys were in second grade. They had been the cause of the leak.

When they were in second grade they avoided one of their teachers, Ms. Grizwell, at all costs. Every opportunity they had they spent in the bathroom. The two old sinks were tiny in comparison to the new bathroom. They even had those old fashioned handles that were made out of porcelain. The right handle read COLD and the left handle read HOT. The handles reminded Harley of the grips on the handlebars of his dad's motorcycle.

On a particular boring day with Sister Germain, the boys were in the bathroom and Harley jumped up on the sink, straddled it, grabbed the faucet handles and pretended to "ride like the wind." Homer watched Harley's face in the mirror over the sink. He jumped on the sink next to Harley and proceeded to "ride along."

They were having the ride of their lives.

"Go right, Homer!" Harley was all smiles as they pushed the left handle away from themselves and pulled the right handle forward. This made the cold water gush from the spigot. They laughed when the water splashed onto them.

Without thinking Homer yelled, "Turn left, Harley!"

The hot water spewed from the faucet before the boys knew what happened. The boys jumped backwards off of the sinks yelling and swearing. They swiped at their pants and stared down into their laps. The crotches of their pants were soaking wet with hot water.

"You dumb sink!" screamed Harley and he kicked it as hard as he could. His foot connected with a pipe under the sink and water started to spew out. The boys knew that they couldn't go back to class with wet pants so they hid in the janitor's closet for the rest of the day. Mr. Hadler, the janitor, did his best to fix the sink but it still leaked. He found an old two handled bucket and put it underneath to catch the drips.

The boy's plan to melt Sister Germain called for a bucket and the boys knew right where to find one, and it was already full of water. Now all they needed was to get Sister Germain into the boys' bathroom.

That's why they needed Rhoda Lee.

Rhoda Lee came flying into the classroom and yelled, "Sister Germ...ain! I smelled smoke comin' from the boys' bathroom!"

"Where's Homer? Where's Harley?" Every time anything happened the teacher immediately thought of the boys.

"They went to the bathroom... *a long time ago*," declared Freddy Lactkey with a devious smile. Freddy loved it when Harley and Homer got into trouble. He even helped it out when he could.

"Frederick, will you please go right to the office and tell Mr. Emeron to meet me in the boy's bathroom?" Sister Germain asked quickly as she flew out of the classroom.

"It will be my pleasure, Sister," smirked Freddy.

Mr. Emeron, the principal, was outside discussing the roof problems of the original part of the school with the janitor, Mr. Hadler, when Freddy reported to the office. The secretary, Mrs. Lancaster, sent Freddy out to find Mr. Emeron. Freddy found the principal staring up at the roof which was just above the window in the boys' bathroom... the same boys' bathroom where Harley and Homer were planning the last details of their plot to melt Sister Germain.

The two boys were facing the doorway right next to the window, which was wide open for ventilation.

"Now you grab one handle and I'll get the other. We'll swing the bucket back and forth real gentle like. I'll start counting and when I yell "THREE" we swing it up and out and we should get her right in the kisser!" Harley giggled as he thought of the nun melting into a smoky pile of black clothes.

Hurried footsteps could be heard getting closer and closer to the door. The boys recognized the sound of black, institutional nun shoes coming at a fast clip. Harley started swinging the bucket gently and Homer followed along.

If you were to ask Homer he would blame Harley. He would tell you that Harley started the count too late. If you asked Harley, he would tell you that Homer just couldn't count. The truth was that Harley started the count when Sister Germain was one step from the doorway. Maybe that was why Homer decided to hurl the bucket at "TWO" instead of "THREE." He just reacted the second he saw Sister Gemain in the doorway.

When you have two people hurl a bucket at the same exact second the water goes straight. When you have one of those people hurl it on the number "TWO" the bucket goes sideways and so does the water. In their case, the water that had been intended to drench Sister Germain and melt her went sideways and straight out the window.

Mr. Hadler had stepped to one side to show Mr. Emeron the loose shingles. Mr. Emeron had stepped with him. That left only Freddy directly under the window when the water, that had been leaking into the bucket and had grown a skim of mold on the top, came raining down onto his face as he looked up. Freddy had the habit of opening his eyes and mouth wide when he saw something out of the ordinary so he was hit in the face full force.

Sister Germain watched as Harley and Homer threw a bucket of water out of the bathroom window. She didn't smell smoke as Rhoda Lee had reported but she was very suspicious about the boy's actions.

"Oh! Hi, Sister Germ ... main! You're probably wondering why we were emptying the bucket. Well Mr. Hadler has been so busy lately with the roof and all that he must have forgot about the bucket under the sink." Harley gave her a smile as Homer continued.

"Harley and me, oh yeah,... Harley and *I*, we just happened ta notice that the bucket was plumb full and so we thought we would help out... just like you taught us to!" Homer grinned ear to ear.

"Can you tell me why you couldn't just empty it down the sink?" Sister Germain's face had a doubtful look.

"Yes, Sister, we can," Homer paused.

"I'm waiting." That was one of her favorite ways to make students sweat.

The stall was just enough time for Harley to respond, "That bucket has been there a long time and some mold was growin' all over the top. You know, the kind that looks like fuzzy puke."

Homer continued, "There was no way that stuff would have gone down the drain so somebody would have had to reach in that sink and pick up that slimy, greenish, yellowish, fuzzy..."

"Enough!" declared the nun as she started turning pale. "Go back to class this instant. I will investigate this matter further. I have the feeling that you boys are not being entirely truthful!"

Homer and Harley returned the bucket and walked into the hall. They saw Mr. Emeron and Freddy walking briskly toward the boys' bathroom. Freddy was leaving a trail of water droplets and was wearing a familiar glob of yellowish green on his head. The boys turned quickly into their classroom and sat down with angelic expressions on their faces.

"Sister Germain! Freddy told me that you needed me

immediately in the boy's bathroom. What is the problem?" inquired the principal.

"It might have been a misunderstanding. It seems that Harley and Homer were trying to assist Mr. Hadler." Sister Germain told him the details with a quizzical look on her face." I have a feeling there might have been more to it than that."

"Perhaps, Sister, all of the work that you have been putting into those two is beginning to have a positive outcome. Don't shortchange yourself, you are an influence on *all* of your students." Mr. Emeron patted Sister Germain on the shoulder.

It was just at that moment that Sister Germain saw Freddy. "Frederick! You are dripping wet! What is that odor? She looked down on his head and saw a strange yellowish, greenish cap. Please remove that cap! I do believe it smells! Get into the bathroom at once and clean up!"

"But Sister..."

"No buts! Just do it!"

Freddy fumed as he tried to clean himself up in the bathroom. He stared into the mirror over the sink and repeated over and over "Harley and Homer, you are dead meat! I'm gonna get you for this!"

When Freddy finally returned to the classroom the discussion was, "How starting rumors can ruin someone's reputation." Rhoda Lee was slumping in her desk.

As Freddy sat down across from Homer, he couldn't help but notice the sneaky expression on Homer's face. When Sister Germain turned to write "Truthfulness" and "Respect" on the board, Homer leaned toward Freddy and said, "Where's your new cap?"

The class had never seen Freddy in a physical fight. He always used verbal abuse to slam kids. The students figured he just flipped out when he lunged for Homer's throat.

After school, Freddy was writing line number sixty-eight of "I will not attack another student when provoked" on the blackboard mumbling all the while, "Harley and Homer, you are dead meat! I'm gonna get you for this!"

CHAPTER TWO

THE UNDERWEAR CAPER

Lola Jean was Homer's mother. Her twin sister was named Lila Jean. Homer's mother talked to her sister on the phone every day. This wouldn't normally be a problem, but Homer's family lived in Missouri and his Aunt Lila Jean lived in New Jersey. Homer's dad, who didn't need an excuse to get angry, yelled at Homer's mom all the time about wasting money. He thought that buying Homer a new pair of sneakers was a waste even when his old ones had a couple of layers of cardboard from cereal boxes lining the inside so he wasn't walking on bare ground.

As if it wasn't bad enough that Homer's mom "Ran up the phone bills 'til they were almost in the poorhouse," Homer's Aunt Lila Jean was "Always puttin' high falootin ideas" into his mom's head. Homer's dad, Hale Hiftman, was not the type of man "ta be wastin' money on nothin" ... not a new dress, or fixin' the house up, or payin for things that his family just didn't need... like new winter coats to replace those that had been worn to threads, or new sneakers because the old ones had holes in the bottoms... there was still plenty of wear left to 'em on the tops. Of course, his idea of "need" was different from Homer's or his mom's or his Aunt Lila Jean's.

Homer's dad *needed* to drink. He used a large part of his weekly paycheck to buy himself a "piece of relaxation" after working all week at Rolley Sanders' Garage and Auto Parts. Hale Hiftman accused Rolley of being a tightwad. That was how he justified slipping small tools, auto parts and various other items into the pockets of his greasy overalls. Not that he sold them to anyone. He kept them in the basement hidden in a large wooden box behind the furnace. The box had a padlock on it, and Hale hid the key on top of a beam that ran the length of the cellar. He always thought that it was *his* little secret, but Homer had found the key when he was seven.

Homer tried his best to keep track of his father's doings. He felt that was the best way to protect his mother. But in the last month Lila Jean had moved back to Missouri after a "nastier than cow manure" divorce. Homer felt that his mom didn't need him anymore, and his dad never did, so he spent most of his time with Harley. Harley filled his life with adventures to keep his mind occupied.

Aunt Lila Jean had to move in with them quickly after the divorce. Homer only heard bits and pieces of the story... something about her ex-husband belonging to the Mafia and sending out a hit man to kill Lila Jean for leaving him. Homer felt a little guilty for hoping that a hit man from the Mafia might actually show up in town. That would be something to see!

Life had become more interesting since his aunt had moved in. She was very different from her sister. Homer's mom was on the quiet and shy side. Aunt Lila said whatever flew into her head. Hale was normally the target of Aunt Lila's sarcastic jabs. That usually lead to Lola's quick defense of her husband. Lola was torn between defending her husband and agreeing with her sister, who tended to say things that rang true.

Even though having his aunt come to live with them was stressful, Homer had to admit to himself that his Aunt Lila was more fun than his parents. She was impulsive, just like Homer. She was also easily talked into things by her favorite nephew, Homer. That's how he managed to get hold of some lacy red underwear, that he and Harley needed for a plan they had.

Every May, their school had a festival in church. This year it was going to be especially grand. The priest had decided to refurbish the statue of Mary. He called upon the members of the parish to contribute to the cause. The restoration began in March, so that the newly painted Mary would be completed by the May Celebration. The unveiling would take place on that day and it would be done by the King of the May Celebration. The Queen of the May Celebration would then place a beautiful wreath of flowers on Mary as a crown.

The May Celebration would begin with a fair in the school cafeteria. Assorted games were played for carnival-like prizes. A bake sale featuring Ms. Reando's famous fudge and divinity, and the ever popular grab bag would draw all of the attention of the younger kids. The adults played Bingo hoping to win handmade quilts, pillowcases with crocheted lace edges, and numerous gift certificates and items from local businesses.

All of the supplies and prizes were brought in by the students. They were given a number of votes for each item they donated. Five pounds of sugar for Ms. Reando could get a student fifty votes. Small trinkets for the grab bag were worth ten votes. Large items like quilts could get a whopping 500 votes.

It was one of those contests that Harley and Homer could never win.

When Mary Louise Hardin's family had bought her the "Queen of May," the boys were not surprised. The Hardin family donated several quilts, lots of sugar and there were thirty Hardin relatives attending the school. A Hardin kid had been in the celebration every year.

The part that made them angry was that Freddy had won, as her escort. They had done their best to persuade, cajole, bribe and bully everyone they could to put all of their votes on a second grader, Elmer Whistle, a short round kid who passed gas frequently. When the boys discovered that Freddy had somehow won, they decided the May Festival was going to be *very different* that year.

"I got the underwear! It's bright red! Nobody will miss seeing *that* on the Mary statue!" Homer was very excited.

"This is gonna be our best plan yet! Nobody'll ever suspect us for this one. After all, where would two guys like us come up with fancy women's underwear!" Harley beamed.

"Now all we have to do is to figure out how we can get the underwear on the statue, so it will stay and for us not to get caught. Did you bring it with you, Homer?"

Homer fumbled in his army surplus knapsack. He gingerly pulled out a bright red bra and matching garter belt. Harley looked at the bra and nodded. He looked at the garter belt with a quizzical look on his face.

"I'm not quite sure how these things work, Homer." Harley looked embarrassed.

"Oh... well these things clip onto ladies' stockings to hold 'em up. One clip in the front and one clip in the back. That's why there are four of 'em 'cuz you know... ladies wear two stockings." Homer was proud to be able to tell Harley something he didn't already know.

"I guess I never even wondered how ladies' stockings were held up. Thanks, Homer, you're a good friend ta tell me without makin' fun and all," Harley said quietly.

"That's what friends are for," whispered Homer. "Besides, I didn't have no idea what they was till I saw Aunt Lila hang this one on the clothesline. She saw me lookin' at it funny, and she told me."

"So how are we gonna git these on a statue?" Harley inquired.

"Well, I figure that we'll have to go into the church the night before the big day." Homer felt great that Harley had put him in charge. "Let's meet in the church that night. We'll come for Perpetual Help Devotions and hide in a pew until everybody leaves. After the priest locks up, we'll give 'er a try. You bring a flashlight, and I'll bring the... um... stuff." He pointed to his knapsack.

The boy's mothers were pleased to hear that the boys wanted to go to an extra church service—a little suspicious maybe—but still pleased. Maybe Mr. Emeron was right. The boys were learning some good things from Sister Germain.

That night the boys crouched down in the pew until the coast was clear. They snuck up to the five-foot Mary statue, that stood on a three-foot wooden base, and pulled off the white sheet that had been placed over the new and improved Mary... the sheet that Freddy would remove at the May Celebration.

"Now, when I get up there on that wooden base that Mary

is standing on, you hand me the bra first," Homer whispered to Harley.

Harley aimed the flashlight beam carefully as Homer climbed up and stood teetering on the edge of the base Mary rested on. Homer threw one arm around Mary's neck and whispered to Harley, "There's not as much room up here as I thought. I don't think that I can hang on and get that underwear on her at the same time. You better climb up, too."

"I don't think that I can climb up there and hold the flashlight at the same time," Harley said.

"Stick the flashlight in your pants. We won't need the light until you get up here anyways." Homer watched as Harley stuck the bright flashlight in the front of his pants. The front of his jeans had a soft glow.

The two boys stood on each side of Mary, balancing by holding onto Mary, Homer with an arm around her neck, and Harley gripping the nose of the statue.

"This might be harder than we figured," Harley whined.

"Naw," stated Homer. "Just hand me the bra."

"You *didn't* tell me ta bring up the underwear," Harley stated matter-of-factly.

"Aw, Harley. Do I have to think of everything? Maybe you could just reach down and get the bag. "

The boys both heard a slight crunching sound as Harley leaned over to get the bag and fell. He sat up at the foot of Mary with the light from the flashlight spilling out of his pants just enough for him to see a plaster nose in his hand.

"Oh Lord!" Harley exclaimed. He held up Mary's plaster nose to show Homer.

"Ah, Harley ... you done broke the mother of Jesus Christ! We're goin' ta hell for sure now." The boys both quickly made the sign of the cross. They looked up at Mary for forgiveness. They decided that if they were going to hell anyway, a few more small infractions wouldn't hurt.

They would figure out what to do about Mary's nose later. They worked on the underwear first. They discovered that they could indeed, put a bra on a statue even if there were no real arms sticking out for the straps. It amazed the boys that

Aunt Lila Jean and Mary were both a size 36C.

The garter belt was a problem, though. The Mary statue did not exactly have a waist. The statue was sort of column shaped. Mary was the same size from the neck down to the feet. The garter belt would not fit around the waist of the statue. Harley improvised by using a large safety pin that held his pants together after he had lost a button. Another problem arose when the garter belt kept riding up on the statue until it was even with the red lacy bra. Homer fixed that by carefully leaning the statue over, the plaster Mary was not that heavy. When Homer tilted Mary ever so carefully, Harley pulled the elastic strips down and slipped the clips under the statue. It did not seem very sturdy, but like Homer said, "It only has ta last for a few hours. Just long enough for Freddy to pull off the sheet. Sister Germ'll see it and collapse with a heart attack."

"Now for the nose," said Homer. "How many Band-Aids do you have on ya?"

"Well... I got one on my arm from fallin' off my bike, and one on my heel 'cuz of my shoes bein' too big, and one on my..."

"Just start handin' 'em over. They're the plain ones right? The ones that look like skin?" inquired Homer.

Harley nodded and started with the one on his arm, picking gingerly at the corner of the Band-Aid.

"Dang it, Harley, just rip the sucker off!" Homer heard a stifled yelp and reached down to get the first of six Band-Aids from Harley that would hold Mary's nose in place at a slight angle.

The May Celebration of Mary always brought out the majority of the congregation. The church was packed as Mary Louise Hardin, dressed in a long gown the color of lime sherbet, was escorted down the aisle by Frederick Lactkey, who was dressed in a suit and bow tie, and had slicked back his hair.

Harley and Homer were seated in the third pew up front, an emergency exit to their right. They wanted a good view with a good getaway.

Sister Germain sat in the pew in front of them, a little to

the left. They had chosen the perfect seats to watch as Freddy stepped up on the small portable staircase that Mr. Hadler, the custodian, had built just for the occasion. He had even painted it white with pink rose decals. Freddy marched up perfectly and climbed the steps to remove the white sheet.

"Where was that staircase when we needed it!" said Homer a little too loudly.

Sister Germain twisted around. "Shhhh!" She gave the boys the evil eye.

When the organist stopped playing "On This Day Oh Beautiful Mary" Freddy reached up and ceremoniously pulled the covering from the statue. At first the congregation was silent. It took everyone a couple of seconds to realize that Mary wore a new wardrobe that was inappropriate. The eyes of the stunned audience traveled up and down the statue pausing at the flaming red lace bra, the matching garter belt, and the nose that was crooked and positioned to the right.

Because their eyes were riveted on Sister Germain, Harley and Homer missed seeing Mary Louise Hardin faint at the sight of an x-rated Mary. Freddy tried to help but became entangled in the white sheet and ended up falling right on top of Mary Louise.

At that exact second Sister Germain jumped up and ran to help Mary Louise and Freddy. At the same time she reached down to pick up Freddy off of Mary Louise, the clips of the garter belt under the statue snapped loose with such force that the undergarment went sailing through the air and wrapped itself around the ceiling fan. Sister Germain screamed as the garter belt flew. The audience looked up at the fan and watched the red undergarment go round and round. Sister Germain looked up too. Then she fainted dead away right on top of Freddy, who was now trapped between Mary Louise Hardin and Sister Germain, his bow tie twisted sideways.

"Wow, Homer! You think Sister Germain is dead?!" asked Harley with slight guilt.

"If she is, this is the one plan that worked!" Homer said with a smile. "Let's go make sure."

Harley and Homer raced to Sister Germain. They were the

first to arrive because the priest was still watching the garter belt spin on the fan.

Sister Germain was face up on the pile of bodies. Her arms were stretched out and the cloth of her black habit hid Freddy entirely, who was face down on top of Mary Louise. None of them looked alive.

Homer leaned over the nun and gingerly picked up her wrist to check her pulse. The congregation had a good view of this scene and it *looked* like the boys were being very concerned and helpful. People didn't realize that Harley and Homer had ulterior motives for checking the nun's vital signs.

Sister Germain responded to Homer's touch. She began moaning. She opened her eyes and said, "Harley? Homer?"

By this time, Father Stonear was standing above the boys and watching what he believed was a true miracle. Harley and Homer were the last people on earth that he thought would respond so quickly and lovingly to Sister Germain's unfortunate dilemma. He smiled as he blessed the boys.

When Sister Germain was helped to her feet, Freddy rolled off of Mary Louise, his bow tie was still vertical and his forehead was bleeding slightly from where it hit one of Mary Louise's front teeth. Freddy touched his forehead and felt the wet blood. He gazed up at Harley and Homer with a panicked look in his eyes.

"AHHHH! I'm dying!" screamed Freddy.

"Nah," said Harley. "Ya just got a little cut on your head."

"Do you have a Band-Aid?" whimpered Freddy.

"I'm plumb out," said Harley looking up at Homer with a smirk. "But I just happen ta know where ta find six of 'em."

CHAPTER THREE

MURDER ON THE MASON FARM

Harley hated the smell in the basement. He had always hated it. But the smell was better than listening to his mom swear and curse about his dad. With his bed right next to the old coal furnace, Harley was insulated from her loud, drunken voice and her bitter cold emotions about his dad, Riley Hauk.

Harley took the brunt of all of this from his mother because his dad wasn't there to hear it. Riley Hauk was back in the penitentiary for violating his parole. Someone had told the cops that Riley had bought a gun. The truth was that Harley's dad had bought several guns, but one is all it took to put him away for ten more years. At that rate, Harley figured that his dad might get out in time to see him graduate from high school, especially if Harley kept flunking every three years.

Harley and his mom, April Mae, lived with his grandfather Earl. Earl slept on the first floor, April Mae slept in the attic space and Harley hid away in the basement. This separation probably kept them all from killing each other over the years.

Earl got a pension check from the railroad, but it never seemed to be enough to feed and clothe his daughter and grandson and have enough left over for a little bag of chewing tobacco. He had warned his only daughter about the likes of Riley Hauk, but it had fallen on deaf ears. Now his only grandson was bitter and filled with hate for a father he barely knew. Maybe that was why the boy had a knack for getting into trouble... like father, like son.

The guns that Riley Hauk had hidden before the sheriff drove him to jail were in a crawl space under the back porch. There must have been twenty boxes of ammunition stored away with the guns. Harley often wondered what his dad had in mind to do with all of that firepower if he hadn't landed back in the hoosegow. They had been wrapped in a piece of heavy, striped canvas awning and tied with twine. Just like Homer found his father's secret by snooping, so did Harley. He frequently took the guns to his bedroom in the basement and cleaned and oiled them. After a while he had taught himself to shoot pretty well, especially with the old .22 hex barreled rifle.

Grandpa Earl knew about Harley's fascination with the guns and tried on occasion to get the boy interested in something else. He was teaching Harley all he knew about engines, just like he had taught his son-in-law Riley. His grandson was quick to pick it up, much quicker than his dad. Earl liked to believe that *his* genes had something to do with it.

A 12-guage shotgun had come in handy the past year. Harley could bag a squirrel or two and that helped the food situation. He had even ventured into bird hunting. He convinced Homer to go with him one summer morning to get quail for dinner. His shooting skills were improving but he still needed the spray pattern of a shotgun to hit a small bird on the wing.

"Now, Homer, you ain't had much practice with a gun so I'll do the shootin' and you'll do the flushin'," Harley stated matter-of-factly.

Homer had no idea what this meant but he would do just about anything to be able to prove to Harley that he could handle a gun, if given half a chance.

When the boys came to the clearing about a mile in back of the old Mason farm, Harley stopped at the edge to give instructions to Homer.

"Here ya go, Homer, I brought ya a hat ta pull down over your hair. That red mop of yours would warn those birds two miles off." Harley pulled a brown knit hat out of the bag that held the ammunition. There was a marshmallow stuck to the hat. He handed the hat to Homer who popped the marshmallow into his mouth. Harley proceeded to put a shell filled with bird shot into the chamber of the shotgun.

"Now you walk through this tall Johnson Grass and flush out the birds. I know a covey of quail lives in here cause I've been watchin' 'em for a couple of weeks." Harley closed the ammo bag and then noticed the look on Homer's face.

The orange curly hair was sticking out all around Homer's face like a halo and his eyes were larger than usual.

"You mean that all I git to do is walk out in the field? When does the shootin' part begin?" Homer asked with a hang dog look.

"The shootin' starts just as soon as you walk out inta the grass and flush out the birds. The quail will take off just as soon as you scare them out. That's when I start shootin'," Harley explained.

"Now wait just a minute Harley," Homer said in a nervous voice. "You are behind me and you start shootin' as soon as the birds take off? That sounds to me like you would be aimin' in my direction with a shotgun full of bird shot!"

"That's about it, Homer," said Harley.

"I'm not that stupid, Harley Hauk! I ain't gonna stand right in front of your target and let you shoot at me!" Homer's face was red, either from anger or heat. Wearing a brown knit hat in warm weather can make a person sweat like a cold soda bottle on a hot summer day.

"Homer, for God'sake, you're not gonna stand there and let me shoot you, 'cuz you'll already be on the ground!" Harley expected to see a look of relief on his friend's face, instead he saw pure panic.

"You brought me out here to kill me?!! After all we've been through together?!!" and with that Homer did an about face and started running.

"Stop, Homer! I ain't gonna kill you! You don't understand!" Harley screamed at the back of Homer but it didn't do any good. The single blast from the gun into the air stopped Homer in his tracks. He turned to face his friend, who he believed was about to shoot him dead.

Harley put the shotgun gently on the ground. Then he backed up a couple of feet and smiled.

"I ain't gonna shoot you, Homer. Honest ta God. Your job is ta walk out in the field. The second you see or hear quail, then you drop flat on the ground. *Then* I shoot."

It took a while for Harley to explain to Homer about flushing out quail. He had convinced Homer that he was not going to kill him by giving him some less-than-fresh marshmallows that he had dumped in with the ammo. The marshmallows tasted slightly metallic. Homer could always be bought with food.

The boys proceeded to stalk the small birds that many folks knew as "bob-whites" because of their call. Harley explained to Homer that they were the same birds that they frequently saw crossing a road in a single file.

All in all, it was quite the learning experience for Homer. It was too bad that it ended on an unfortunate note.

* * *

Old man Mason was as deaf as a doorknob so he didn't react to the shotgun blasts in his back field. It was his wife Helen, who couldn't *see* worth beans, who called Police Chief Davis to report a murder in the back cornfield that had lay fallow for five years. Her husband Charlie had not been up to plowing and planting after he turned eighty-five so he let the field go and it had been taken over by tall Johnson Grass.

"Why of course I'm sure, Chief Davis! That's why I'm callin' you! You'd best git right out here before that maniac shoots somebody else!" Helen was getting frustrated with the chief. Her eyesight might not be as good as it used to be, but she sure as hell knew a murder when she saw one.

"Well, some tall guy with black hair just shot a short man with brown hair. It sounded to me as if he was usin' a shotgun. And as if that wasn't bad enough he shot the man again when he was down on the ground... at close range no less!"

She listened to the phone and then replied, "I am not fool enough ta go out there and chase no murderin' maniac! I'm an old woman, for God'sake! You just git yourself out here and do your job! I'm lockin' our door and hidin' in the root cellar."

With that said, Helen escorted her husband one step at a time to the root cellar, even though Charlie had no idea what was going on.

Chief Davis was on his way to the Mason farm when he passed Harley Hauk and Homer Hiftman. The boys waved at the police chief and he pulled over. They had seen him coming and had stashed the gun and bag filled with ammo, two dead quail, and some marshmallows behind a couple of sumac bushes. Homer stuffed the brown knit cap into his back pocket, releasing his wild, curly, red hair.

Police Chief Davis knew the boys and their families. He had gone to school with Harley's dad Riley. He had even dated Homer's mom, Lola Jean, a couple of times when they were juniors, right before she dropped out of school to take care of her sick mother.

He had made several "official" visits to Homer's house after neighbors had called in to report that Hale was getting out of hand. He would drive Lola Jean and Little Homer to a cousin's house to spend the night until Hale had a chance to sober up.

Riley Hauk had been sent back to prison because of evidence that Chief Davis had come upon while cruising the back county roads. He caught Riley red handed buying a gun from Junior Peaser, another parolee who also was sent back to the pen.

The chief felt sorry for the boys. He thought that they were headed for trouble and that was why he had tried to befriend them, to turn them onto the right path. Most things they did were just stunts like many other boys pulled. It didn't seem right that the boys had to live with the sins of their fathers hanging over them.

"You boys happen ta see anyone out by the Mason farm?" asked the chief.

"No sir. We ain't been out that away. We was down by the crick catchin' crawdads to go fishin'." Harley had learned from his dad to always cover his tracks, especially when it came to officers of the law.

"Why?" asked Harley.

"Aw, it probably ain't nothin'. Helen Mason phoned in to report a murder in the old cornfield behind their house. Seems like a tall guy with black hair killed a short guy with brown hair. Shot him once and then shot him again when he was down, or at least that's what Helen claims. Last time she called she said she saw a UFO land next to her vegetable garden. That turned out to be an electrical truck that had shorted out. All of its lights were goin' off. It scared the daylights out of old Helen." Chief Davis looked first at Harley and his black hair and then at Homer and his wild red curls. *Naw, couldn't be* he thought to himself. He also looked for a bait bucket. When he saw none he became suspicious again.

"Where did you say you boys been?" he asked more sternly.

"We've been at the crick catchin' crawdads," Homer stated.

"Where's your bait bucket?" the chief asked as one eyebrow went up.

"It was the durndest thing," Harley began. "That ol' bucket got a big hole in it when Homer decided to chuck a rock at it. Now we have to go and get another one and start all over, thanks to dumb Homer here."

"Who you callin' dumb?! You're the one who said that I couldn't hit it." With that Homer pushed Harley and both boys tumbled to the ground.

"All right, all right, break it up you two." The chief lifted up the boys. "No more of that!" Harley and Homer stared at each other like two tom cats.

"If you happen ta see any thing out of the ordinary, give me a holler. I'll be at the Mason's." He looked at the boys one last time.

The two friends had a hard time trying not to laugh. They had discovered years ago that if they started fighting, the adults would forget what the boys had said or done to get in trouble to begin with.

After the squad car pulled away, Homer grabbed Harley's arm, looked him straight in the eye and said, "Can you believe that we just missed out on seein' a real live murder! Let's go back! I'll bet there'll be police cars and State Marshal's and maybe the FBI!"

Harley picked up the brown knit hat that had fallen out of Homer's pocket and handed it to him shaking his head, "How 'bout another marshmallow, Homer?

CHAPTER FOUR

GHOSTS, A SPIDER MONKEY AND DYNAMITE

The small town the boys lived in had few entertainment opportunities, and the ones that it did have, like the Rosemont Theater, cost money. In the summer after the boys had finished "a rough year" with Sister Germain in the fourth grade, they fished, hunted and prowled the woods. It seemed to happen that every time Harley and Homer were most bored, one of the two friends would come up with an idea that sounded exciting but did not quite work out the way they planned. Take for example Harley's idea to somehow get rid of the ghosts in the cemetery.

The fact was that the cemetery was not haunted. The sounds that came from amid the tombstones at night were those of a spider monkey named Mort. The town grave digger, Droop Voicy, had acquired Mort from the nanny of a very rich family. While the parents were away their children had mail ordered a monkey and the nanny discovered that it could not be returned. Mr. Voicy helped her out by taking the monkey to the cemetery where he lived. He kept the spider monkey in the mausoleum of the rich family. The monkey was quite at home in the decorative cement building. He didn't ever know that the building was where they stored dead bodies until the ground was thawed enough in the spring to bury the bodies. It had never contained a body. The rich family was not only rich, they were very healthy as well.

"Come on, Homer, we're gonna prove ta everyone in this town that we can get rid of all of the ghosts and haints and banshees in this cemetery. I got a cross, holy water, garlic, and if that don't

work I got me some silver-lookin' bullets and my dad's pistol."
Harley grinned from ear to ear. He knew Homer was dying to
try his dad's pistol after going quail hunting with him.

"I promised my mom that I wouldn't get inta no more
trouble. She almost killed me after we sawed down that
big oak in front of the courthouse to build the ark." Homer
sounded whiny.

"Hell, Homer, it had rained for seven days and nights. We
were just doin' what that holy geezer Noah did, and they
wrote a whole chapter about him in the bible." Harley looked
at Homer and saw him roll his eyes. "All right, then, you just
be a lily-livered, sap-suckin' baby. I'm gonna show all of the
folks in town that I'm the ONLY one in town brave enough to
go head-to-head with the living dead, and I'll do it with ya or
without ya!" Harley turned his back and pretended to storm
off.

"Oh, Harley, all right I'll come with ya, but ya gotta promise
me that I can shoot the gun when the ghosts come out." Harley
turned and smiled at Homer, cinching the deal.

"Now it's startin' ta get dark so we best find us a place ta camp.
We don't want that crazy ol' grave digger ta find us." Harley
led the way up the hill. When he spotted the mausoleum for
the richest family in town he stopped and stared.

"Holy shit, Homer, just look at this place! Those folks have
so much money that they can afford two whole houses, one
for when they're alive and one for when they're dead. Let's
camp right behind here. It'll be the closest we'll get ta livin' in
a rich neighborhood."

The sun was just below the horizon when Homer stopped
and whispered to Harley, "Listen! Do ya hear somethin?"

"Ah, Homer, don't go gettin' yourself spooked. It ain't even
totally dark yet! Help me get this tent up. This ground is solid
rock and I cain't put the stakes in. Hand me somethin' to
pound these things in with."

"I cain't find no hammer, Harley. Didn't ya bring a
hammer?!"

"Hell, no, I didn't bring no hammer. I was the one who was
in charge of the anti-spook apparatus, remember? You were

the one who was in charge of everything else."

Homer started to rummage through the knapsack that they had brought to survive the night. He inventoried it out loud: "An old horse blanket...."

"In case it gets cold," grunted Harley, still trying to get the tent stake in the ground.

"Ten cans of Vienna Sausages."

"That's six for me and four for you 'cuz you don't like 'em as much as I do," stated Harley.

"Then I get most of the beef jerkies 'cuz I like 'em more than you do," quipped Homer. He took out the beef jerkies and put four of the five, foot long pieces of dried meat to the side. "Harley... why in the hell did ya bring a can of hair spray?"

"'Cuz I didn't have a flame thrower! Some of these monster types is afraid of fire so I figured that if we came across one that we couldn't kill with silver bullets we'd just torch'em. I saw it on TV. You just press down on the hair spray nozzle, light a match, and instant flame thrower." Harley had a confident look on his face.

Harley was still tryin' to get the tent stakes into the ground when Homer said, "Look it, Harley! Two sticks of dynamite, you can blast a hole in the ground to soften it up a bit!"

"I found it in my dad's ammo stash. That dynamite is a last resort. I figure we only use it if a banshee tries to drag us into the grave with 'em." Homer gazed at Harley with admiration.

Next, Homer brought out a large wooden cross that opened up and held two candles and the holy oils of Extreme Unction, for the sacrament for the dying. "I guess this is just in case some spook gets us for good. It is nice to know that ya thought of makin' sure that we'd get to heaven. That would be enough to make Sister Germain keel over."

Five garlic bulbs, three onions, a kitchen box of matches, four socks that didn't have mates, two long red candles, and a large bag of fried pork rinds came out of the bag next. "Don't you get inta those, Homer. Those pork rinds are for breakfast," Harley warned.

In the bottom was the pistol with a box of ammo. Homer took it out and caressed it. "Blast it, Homer, would ya find me somethin' ta pound these stakes in with. It ain't gettin no lighter out here ya know."

Homer repacked the knapsack. He put the gun back into the bag reverently. He started to look around the area for something to use as a hammer. He came across a perfectly square rock about six inches with some kind of engraving on it. He had to pry it out of the ground with the wooden cross. "Here, Harley, whack it with this."

Harley studied the rock and then dropped it. "Holy shit, Homer! That rock is a grave marker or somethin'! That's the last thing you want ta do in a graveyard is to offend the dead! Somethin' like that is just enough ta piss off a banshee!"

"Hell, Harley, how was I supposed ta know that it was a grave marker. Isn't it awful small ta be a tombstone?"

"Homer, ya got ta be real careful when you're dealin' with the living dead. Dead folks take things real serious. Now just take one of these stakes and start ta dig a hole so we can get the tent up."

Homer joined Harley and started to dig. Just as Homer jabbed the stake into the earth the boys heard a small whimper. They turned to look at each other.

"I'll get the gun!" said Homer.

"No, Homer, ya cain't jump to no conclusions. That just might be a hooty owl or somethin'."

The whimper was louder then, and it seemed to be coming from inside of the mausoleum.

"I'll get the gun!" said Harley.

"Wait, Harley! Look!" Homer said in a frantic whisper.

Both boys looked to where Homer was pointing. "Get down, Homer! That's the old grave digger. If he finds out we're here, we're in deep shit!"

Droop Voicy walked slowly to the door of the mausoleum as he did every night. Mort, the spider monkey, was waiting anxiously for his nightly run. The grave digger inserted a key into the lock and went inside. The boys could hear soft mumbling, and in the growing darkness the boys could see the shadows of the grave digger and what appeared to be a small child holding his hand leaving the tomb of the dead. The childlike creature screeched and took off running, climbing quickly up the nearest tree. Harley clamped a hand over Homer's mouth.

"It's worse than I thought Homer... he's one of them. The old grave digger is one of the living dead!" Homer grabbed Harley around the neck so tight that Harley could barely breathe. After the two shadows disappeared around the corner Harley took his hand from Homer's mouth, but Homer did not let go of Harley's neck.

"Let's get outa here," whispered Homer desperately.

"We cain't go yet, Homer. We gotta rid this town of this awful affliction. We got to kill these banshees once and for all." Homer knew that when Harley used his John Wayne voice that they were in big trouble.

"How in the hell do ya kill somethin' that's already dead, Harley?! I say we just go get Chief Davis and let him handle this banshee problem. Hell, he gits paid for this kinda stuff!" Homer wanted to leave in the worst way. He started to turn.

"Get the gun Homer." Homer did an about face and grabbed the bag.

"We're goin' in," Harley said matter-of-factly.

Homer gave Harley the hair spray and the cross. He stuffed garlic and onions and matches into every pocket he had. He dragged the bag with one hand as he held the gun out in front of him shakily.

"We're gonna need one of those candles so we can see when we get inside," Harley instructed. Homer fumbled around in the bag and pulled out a red stick with a wick on it.

The door to the mausoleum had been left open and Harley led with Homer trailing behind. The boys inched their way toward the tomb of the dead. Just outside the door, Homer pulled a match from his pocket and held it to the wick.

At the same time that the boys were going into the mausoleum, Mort the spider monkey was watching from a nearby oak tree. Mort seldom saw humans, as Droop hid him whenever possible so no one would discover his secret pet. Mort became curious. He leaped down branch to branch and when he was right behind the boys he let out a welcoming screech.

* * *

Mort had a singed tail and was left deaf in his right ear from the explosion. Droop had to knock him out with hard liquor every time there was a Christian burial, because Mort had developed a god-awful fear of crosses and candles.

Harley and Homer's survival was credited to St. Jude.

Police Chief Davis did not buy their story about afflictions and banshees and the living dead, even though people still reported hearing strange screeching sounds at night. He confiscated all the guns Harley's dad had stashed.

Many of the people in town went by the cemetery to see the mausoleum that had been blown to bits. Some spectators mistook the scattered Vienna sausages, beef jerky and pork rinds for body parts.

CHAPTER FIVE

UP TO THEIR NECKS

Harley and Homer were somewhat subdued after the cemetery episode, or as Brer' Rabbit would have said, "The boys lay low." Chief Davis had come very close to sending the two to Father Flannigan's Home for Wayward Boys. He talked with Mr. Emeron who convinced him that the boys would have a much better year that fall. He was putting them in Sister Frances' fifth grade classroom. She had a reputation for being very strict.

Freddy was always plotting a scheme to get back at Harley and Homer and seeing that the two were watching their every step with Sister Frances, aka, Sister Frankenstein, he figured that it was the perfect time for revenge.

It was a cold January day when St. Rose School began at seven-thirty in the morning. Homer met Harley on the playground by the slide, just like he did on most school mornings.

The dreary winter weather was getting to the boys. They were antsy or as Harley said, "I've got heebie-jeebies." They had stayed out of trouble for four months, if you didn't count several small incidents that they weren't blamed for, like sneaking into school and setting all of the clocks ahead an hour so they could get out of school early. They had forgotten about nuns wearing watches, possibly because as Harley told Homer "Hell, they could hide a bazooka in those clothes."

If the bus driver for their field trip hadn't been a substitute their "extended trip" idea could have gotten them into trouble. Sister Frances usually drove the bus, but she had sprained her right foot falling over a stack of Webster's dictionaries that had been mysteriously placed in the aisle. She had to be driven to the hospital by Father Stonear. The substitute bus driver, Herman McBroom, believed Homer when he told him he knew the way to Cooper's Farm and Animal Excursion, a mere fifteen miles away.

The bus ended up going to Cairo, Illinois, and didn't get back until school was over. The students never told on Homer. It was a good thing that Sister Frances had landed on Freddy when she tripped. He had to go along with Father Stonear to the hospital that day for X-rays. Freddy had retaliated claiming he was fine, but the priest was not about to take chances with the wealthiest family in the school. "Well, if that was one of us, they would have made us clean up the blood and then sent us to detention for makin' a mess," Homer told Harley.

The students loved the ride. There was no one to lead them in prayers, which was Sister Frances' usual way to keep a bus quiet. Harley lead a rousing rendition of "Ninety-Nine Bottles of Beer on the Wall." The substitute driver was so embarrassed about the whole field trip, that he kept everything to himself.

So no one had caught onto those little incidents, even though Sister Frances was suspicious when the students continuously asked for Herman McBroom to be their driver. The boys were ready for action.

* * *

"Well, at least it might snow. They're callin' for six inches by the time school lets out. Let's head for Third Street to do a little sleddin'," Homer suggested.

The boys did not have regular sleds like the other kids. Those things cost money that Harley and Homer didn't have, so they improvised by using an old sheet of plywood. Harley's dad had used it as a ramp to get his motorcycle into the shed out back of Harley's house.

There was no steering mechanism on the plywood, but that made it all the more exciting for them. They just loved being out of control on a steep hill crowded with other sledders.

About ten-thirty the snow began, lightly at first, but by noon it was coming down at a good clip. Harley and Homer had a hard time concentrating on what Sister Frances was talking about. This was not unusual, however. During lunch they were working out the details of their sledding trip when Rhoda Lee sat down at their table. The boys looked up in surprise. After the cemetery incident, kids avoided the boys like stinging nettles.

"Hi, Homer. Is it OK if I sit here?" she asked, ignoring Harley entirely.

Homer was about to tell her to leave when he noticed she had dumped out her lunch bag. He couldn't believe his eyes. There were three sandwiches that were thick with filling. They looked like ham salad, his favorite. She also had fried cheese curls, three packages of Twinkies, and a large piece of chocolate layer cake. Rhoda Lee watched Homer drool.

"Sure," said Homer not taking his eyes off of her banquet in a bag.

After being bribed with the second ham salad sandwich, a large portion of fried cheese curls, three Twinkies and the entire piece of chocolate layer cake, Homer would have taken Rhoda Lee Swampson to Paris and back.

Harley, on the other hand, was skeptical. If it hadn't been for Homer's persistent kicking right in his shins every time he tried to get them out of taking Rhoda Lee with them, Harley would have objected more strongly. When the plans were finalized Homer was looking forward to going with Rhoda Lee because she promised to bring hot chocolate and sugar cookies.

Unbeknown to the three, Freddy Lactkey had been listening to their plans as he sat at the table next to them with his back to them. Elmer Whistle sat with him. Freddy was working on a plan of his own and he convinced or bribed Elmer to help him.

Walking single file back to class with Sister Frances in the lead, Elmer slipped out of his line and positioned himself right behind Harley.

"Hey, Harley. Have you ever gone down Devil's Hill on a sled?" Elmer whispered.

"Shhhh!" shushed Sister Frances without even turning around.

"Devil's Hill?" asked Harley.

"Yeah! Freddy bet me a dollar that you don't have the guts to go down Devil's Hill. I said of course you do and Freddy said that you were a wimp and didn't have the...."

"I hear talking!" scolded Sister Frances.

"I don't even know where this Devil's Hill is," whispered Harley.

"Freddy says it is behind the shoe factory. He says it's the baddest, scariest, wickedest hill around and that he knows that you can't do it 'cuz you're a...."

"Don't make me come back there!" This time sister Frances stopped the line and turned around. Elmer hid behind Harley. She gave the students her fierce face, the one where she squinted her eyes and pressed her lips together. After she was satisfied that the talking had stopped she started down the hall again.

Harley turned around just long enough to say "Tell him I'll be there after school."

There was no Devil's Hill. Freddy had made it up to get Harley and Homer behind the shoe factory. Freddy's dad owned the factory, so Freddy had been there many times. He knew about the large bails of leather scraps behind the factory that sat at the bottom of a treeless hill. Next to the old leather bales was the sewage lagoon where the factory wastes were piped. Those wastes not only included the chemicals used to process the leather, but, also the wastes from the ten bathrooms that were needed for the four hundred employees. Freddy would have just enough time after school to position the bales of leather and hose down the steepest part of the slope with water.

Homer understood perfectly when Harley told him of the change in their plans. Rhoda Lee didn't mind one bit, just so long as she could be with Homer. It took the trio forty-five minutes to gather what they needed and get to the shoe factory. They would have made it sooner, but Rhoda Lee had to wait for her mom to go to the bathroom so she could sneak out the sugar cookies. She had already been questioned about the two lunches that had disappeared that morning, the ones intended for her two little brothers, Sam and Griff. It took ten precious minutes for Rhoda Lee to convince her mother that she knew nothing about the disappearance of the food. She'd think up an excuse for the missing cookies later. Right now Homer was waiting.

The large piece of plywood was being pulled by Harley and pushed by Homer and Rhoda Lee. At the bottom of the hill they saw Elmer Whistle. He didn't say a word, just pointed to Freddy standing at the top watching.

"This is going to be so sweet," Freddy said to himself.

"You call this the baddest, scariest, wickedest hill in town?" questioned Harley breathing a little heavy from the climb.

"It's trickier than you think. The trick is not to run into the bales of leather. You think you're tough enough to do it?" questioned Freddy.

"Yup." said Harley "We'll do 'er." He climbed onto the plywood followed close behind by Homer who held onto Harley's waist and Rhoda Lee who held onto Homer's waist with a bag of cookies and a thermos of hot chocolate wedged in between.

The boys had been sledding on plywood for a number of years. They knew when to lean right or left, when to stick a foot over the edge and drag it to slow down, and most importantly, when to roll off if they needed to in case of an emergency. Rhoda Lee, on the other hand, had never been sledding period, a small fact that she neglected to tell Homer, not that it would have mattered.

Poor Elmer Whistle was an unsuspecting witness to the whole fiasco. He didn't know that Freddy had set up the whole thing, he just wanted the dollar Freddy promised him. He truly believed that Harley Hauk was gutsy enough to do just about anything. It sounded like easy money to him.

The plywood was slow to get started because of the weight of the added passenger, but with a little shove from Freddy it picked up speed rapidly. At first Rhoda Lee was thrilled as a pig in mud to be so close to Homer. The thermos of chocolate felt warm and the cookies smelled sweet nestled between them. These pleasurable feelings lasted for about five seconds.

That's about how long it took the piece of plywood to reach warp speed. Harley put a foot quickly over the side to drag but found that it did not have any friction on the hill Freddy had iced. Homer couldn't be of any assistance because Rhoda Lee had him in a death grip.

A ride that should have lasted at least forty-five seconds was over in fifteen. Things started to go very badly about in the middle of the hill when Homer felt warm liquid on his rear end. He hoped that it was hot chocolate, but with the way Rhoda Lee was screaming he feared the worst.

Elmer Whistle tried to warn them by waving both arms in the air. He gave up, covered both of his eyes with mittened hands, and passed gas. By then it was too late, too late to roll off, too late to try to stop, even too late to pray.

When the plywood hit the sewage lagoon it kind of floated on top for a second. Then it sank like a rock. The three passengers were up to their necks in raw sewage.

Rhoda Lee was suddenly silent holding a bag covered in brown slop.

Homer saw that the thermos still had the lid tightly screwed on. It was not hot chocolate that he had felt. It was the worse thing that had ever happened to him. Then he looked down at the brown sludge that covered his body and thought *maybe not.*

Elmer Whistle didn't know how to react to the three who looked like creatures from the black lagoon so he ran home as fast as he could, farting all the way.

Harley looked up and saw Freddy standing at the top of the hill laughing like a hyena.

CHAPTER SIX

WONDERS NEVER CEASE

Ya got any money, Homer?" Harley asked first thing in the morning at their regular meeting place.

"Nope." Homer was obviously chewing on something.

"Well, can you GET any money?" Harley tried again.

"Nope." Homer popped something else into his mouth. It looked and smelled like a cinnamon roll.

"Homer, would you kindly stop stuffin' your face and listen to me?" Harley yelled.

"I am lishening to you," Homer mumbled through the spicy dough ball he was chewing. "Wan' one?" He held out a small piece of cinnamon roll.

"Dang it, Homer! Did Rodent Lee give you them buns?" Harley asked.

Homer swallowed and answered, "Yeah and there ain't nothin' wrong with 'em. I already ate six." He smiled innocently at Harley.

"I thought that we had an agreement about Rodent Lee! You were going to stay as far away from that girl as you could. It was all her fault that we were up to our necks in shit, or have you forgotten that! It seems them cinnamon rolls have gone to your head!" Harley stared at Homer with his dark eyes.

"Ah, Harley, I don't think you can blame the whole thing on Rhoda Lee. Freddy just tricked us is all. Rhoda Lee ain't so bad as you think, and she cooks real good." Homer popped another piece of roll into his mouth and smiled.

"I have a notion ta let you make the biggest mistake of your life and just suffer from it. 'cuz if you start gettin' in thick with

Rodent Lee everyone in school is gonna avoid you like skunk piss." Harley was having trouble with the idea of Homer having another friend, especially a friend the likes of Rhoda Lee Swampson. Homer knew what Harley was thinking.

"You're still my best friend, Harley, and you always will be. It would be awful nice though... if you would learn how to cook." Homer grinned at Harley and they laughed at the idea of Harley cooking. They were still laughing when they entered the school building.

"What's so funny? Did you two look in the mirror?" quipped Freddy.

"Freddy, you don't know the difference between a mirror and a window. We looked through the window and saw your sorry lookin' face and we've been laughin' ever since," said Homer as Freddy marched off in a huff.

"What do you need money for?" asked Homer.

"Just lunch as usual," said Harley.

"We can invite Rhoda Lee to sit with us," Homer suggested.

"I'd rather starve," Harley spat back.

When the boys entered the classroom they heard mumbling among the students. Rhoda Lee ran up to them and whispered, "Did you hear the news? Mr. Glover the music teacher has disappeared. Nobody knows what happened. He might have died or somethin'. They ain't tellin'. All we know is that there is a new guy startin' today."

"That's great," said Harley in a disappointed voice.

The boys had actually liked going to music because Mr. Glover was either deaf or just didn't give a tinker's damn about teaching. His was the one class that Harley and Homer attended every day. They sat in the back of the classroom and talked to each other the whole time. They had even mastered the technique of singing conversations. While the rest of the class sang hymns or spirituals or whatever in Latin, Harley and Homer sang to each other such things as *Heum isum asum deafus asum treeum*. Poor Mr. Glover smiled as he watched the boys always participating in the songs. He thought that he was the one teacher who had a positive influence on the troublemakers. They were always cooperative and had near perfect attendance.

The students were anxious to go to music right before lunch. Rumors were rampant about Mr. Glover, everything from his getting hit by a train he didn't hear... to alien abduction. They hoped that the substitute could shed some light on the subject... and he most certainly did.

In huge writing on the blackboard was the name "Mr. Dino Draggi." In front of the class stood a man dressed entirely in black, except for the expensive crisp white shirt with DD monogrammed on the collar. His shoes were the Italian leather kind that cost more than Homer's dad made in a month.

The students stood around with gaping mouths. This was definitely not your ordinary substitute. The name written on the blackboard was foreign and to top it all off he gave the students both his first and his last name. Nuns only gave you their first name, and lay teachers only gave you their last names. Giving students both names was never heard of.

"Youse kids sit in ya seats, and do it now if ya know what's good for ya!" Mr. Draggi said with great authority or as Harley said later, "In an accent that was definitely Mafia."

"My name is Mister Draggi. I'm here ta teach youse guys music."

"What happened to Mr. Glover?" asked Freddy.

"You ain't gonna see him no more," Mr. Draggi said ominously.

"Ever?" asked Freddy.

"That's what I told youse. Now sit down. I took the liberty of bringing wit me some of the best music ever sung by the best singer in the world." Mr. Draggi paused reverently. "Now youse kids listen up so's youse can sing like Frank Sinatra."

"But Mr. Glover was teaching us a new Gregorian Chant, in Latin!" Freddy informed the teacher.

"That Gregorian stuff is nothin' compared to Frank Sinatra, and like I told youse Mr. Glover ain't coming back no more! He's fini', gone, out of the picture so's ta speak. I'm here to teach youse good music and that's what I'm gonna do."

Freddy looked as if he had been slapped in the face. Mr. Glover always used Freddy's singing as an example of high quality to the class.

Mr. Draggi then turned to write something else on the board. When his right arm reached up his black suit coat flapped open and Homer saw a bulge under his jacket. When Homer, Harley and Rhoda Lee started piecing things together later, it all added up to trouble.

"Did you hear the way Mr. Draggi talks! He sounds like a mobster! He dresses like a mobster! " Harley started the list of strange characteristics of Mr. Dino Draggi.

"And I'm sure that he had a leather holster holding a .38 special under his jacket!" Homer added.

All of the descriptions of Mr. Dino Draggi lead Homer and Harley to believe that Mr. Dino Draggi was a hit man, sent by the mob to kill Homer's Aunt Lila Jean for leaving her husband.

Rhoda Lee was not convinced until they left school at the end of the day. The huge black car with the New Jersey license plates parked in the faculty parking lot was what cinched it for her. She tried to console Homer with words, as she was all out of food.

"You cain't be for sure that Mr. Draggi is a mobster. After all, he did know a *little* about music," she tried not to stare at the car.

"Yeah, Frank Sinatra tunes. *Everybody* knows that he's in tight with the mob," Homer stated sadly.

"Well if he was here to get rid of your aunt why would he take a job as a music teacher?" asked Rhoda Lee. Without food Rhoda Lee lost some of her appeal to Homer.

"Don't you know nothin'! It's his cover! This way he can get people ta think that he is just a harmless music teacher. He'll gain their confidence and then... POW... it's all over but the cryin'." Harley was nodding in agreement with Homer.

The three agreed that it was not a good idea to tell Homer's Aunt Lila Jean quite yet. They were going to watch Mr. Draggi like a hawk and start digging for information.

It was Rhoda Lee's idea to question Sister Frances. "She'll have to tell us the truth 'cuz if nuns lie they will die and go to hell right on the spot."

"Rhoda Lee's got a good point, Harley. If she lies, then we

get rid of Sister, Pain in Our Necks, Frankenstein. If she tells us the truth, then we can report Mr. Draggi to the Feds." Homer smiled at Harley.

The next morning before school Rhoda Lee went into the classroom early. Sister Frances was busy writing the day's work on the board.

"Excuse me, Sister Frances, but could I please ask your advice about something?" Rhoda Lee was looking somewhat better this morning, she had on clean socks and her hair was shining. As a matter of fact, thought Sister Frances, Rhoda Lee had been looking better for a couple of weeks now ... ever since she had taken up company with Homer Hiftman.

"If this question has anything to do with your newly found relationship with Homer Hiftman, you can just save your breath. Nothing good can possibly come from it." She turned her back on Rhoda Lee.

"Why no Sister, I just wanted your opinion about the special card that we are making for Mr. Glover." Rhoda Lee was now convinced that this nun was a witch, too. How else would she know about her feelings for Homer? Homer didn't even know.

"Card for Mr. Glover?" inquired the nun with her back still turned.

"Yes Ma'am. We would like to send a card to Mr. Glover to tell him we are sorry for whatever is wrong with him. Our problem is we don't know exactly what to say. Should we say "Get Well," "Sorry About Your Accident," "Sympathy at This Time of Great Loss," or "Enjoy Your Retirement"?

Sister Frances turned around slowly. She looked Rhoda Lee right in the eye. Rhoda Lee tried to look sincere. She smiled at the nun.

"I am pleased about your intentions and I am sure that Mr. Glover would be, too, but a card is not necessary. Just remember to keep Mr. Glover in your prayers." She said it in her "end of discussion" tone of voice. She pointed to the clock indicating that Rhoda Lee needed to go back outside until the official start of school.

Rhoda Lee left with no more information than when she

started. She met Harley and Homer at the slide.

"Well? What'd she say?" Harley inquired.

"She said not to send a card," Rhoda Lee said softly.

"That's it? Just 'Don't send a card'? What kind of information is that? I thought you said you could make her talk," said Harley disappointedly.

"She did tell me something else. She said to keep Mr. Glover in our prayers. That at least sounds like he is still alive." Rhoda Lee looked sheepishly at Harley.

"No it doesn't! People keep prayin' for people even if they've been dead for years. My grandmother has been praying for her sister Althea for as long as I've known her. I asked her about it once and she said that she will pray for Great Aunt Althea 'til the day she dies. Seems her sister got into so much trouble that it made their mother so sick she died. Grandma called it Nerve Sickness." Harley paused and then whispered, "She told me 'cuz she thinks I'm givin' my mom Nerve Sickness... that's why she drinks so much." Harley cast his eyes down. He seldom talked about his family troubles to anyone but Homer.

"Well, I guess we don't know no more now than we did before." Homer stated the obvious.

"There is one thing for sure, Sister Frances *does* know something about Mr. Glover, and she won't tell. That means that it must be bad or else she could tell us." Rhoda Lee was right about that. Sister Frances did indeed know something about Mr. Glover. As she peeked out her window to spy on the three students she was wondering how long it would take before someone let the cat out of the bag about Mr. Glover. At her morning break she went into the principal's office to discuss the matter behind closed doors with Mr. Emeron.

Meanwhile the students did not give up.

* * *

Homer's Aunt Lila Jean did not have a clue about the suspicions of Homer and his friends. She was making a new life for herself after her ugly divorce. Coming back to the land of her birth was somewhat depressing for her, but she was making the best of it. Lila had always believed that she was meant to do greater things. In order to accomplish her goals she believed that she needed to be in a big city. That was how she ended up in New Jersey married to a flashy man who threw his money around. He threw some her way and she was hooked. She would tell her sister that she had no idea he was connected to the Mafia, but that was a lie. She not only knew about his relationship with Tony Balero, the mob boss, she enjoyed living the high life with a criminal... while it lasted.

Now living in this one-horse town, Lila tried to make the best of it. She just couldn't seem to find anything decent to wear at the shops in town. Lila solved her dilemma, however, by making her own clothes. Her sense of fashion was noticeable in a town where most women wore jeans. Lila flounced around in long flowing dresses and large hats with flowing ribbons. She wrapped vibrant feather boas around her neck. She stood out like a peacock in a flock of sparrows. Her new venture was even bringing in a little money though. Folks would admire this or that piece of clothing and Lila would sew it up... for a price.

It was while watching his Aunt Lila pinning together a Hawaiian shirt on her dressmaker's dummy one evening, when the idea popped right into his head. The life-sized form, that was only a head and torso might just do... with a little work. He couldn't wait to tell Harley and Rhoda Lee.

Homer was the first to arrive at their morning meeting place by the slide.

"I got the perfect plan to get rid of Mr. Dino Draggi and save Aunt Lila Jean!" He was so excited that he was shaking. "All we have to do is kill off Aunt Lila Jean and then Mr. Draggi will leave town." Homer noticed the wide eyes of his friends. "I don't mean REALLY kill her off, I mean we just have to convince Mr. Draggi that she is dead."

His partners in crime listened carefully, nodding and smiling. They began hashing out the details. They thought the plan was perfect. The dressmaker's dummy that Aunt Lila had was the perfect size, they only needed to make it look as much like Lila Jean as they could. Most of the supplies they needed were very accessible to Homer: a hat with feathers, a colorful boa, and a dress. They only had to find a long rope, a set of arms and legs, and someone to pull the fire alarm at the right time.

Harley got the rope from his grandfather. Elmer Whistle offered to pull the fire alarm after he was bribed with one of Rhoda Lee's special lunches and when he was losing his nerve, threatened by Harley who was at least six inches taller and had a reputation, already laced with guns and dynamite.

The arms and legs were not as easy to get. Rhoda Lee convinced her little sister Shirley to play hospital and they used her sister's doll as the patient. The doll was one of those large ones that stood about the same height as Shirley who was six years old. The arms and legs might have looked a little short, but short arms and legs were better than no arms and legs at all. After all, the only parts that would really show were the hands and feet. The doll was made of tough plastic. It required a hacksaw to amputate the limbs. Rhoda Lee convinced Shirley to wear a surgical mask—an old dishcloth—over her face to avoid giving Dolly an infection. The mask was pulled tightly over Shirley's eyes, looped around her head and tied in the front with the knot strategically placed in her mouth. Rhoda Lee had planned it well, so Shirley could not *see* the removal of her doll's arms and legs and could not *scream* if she did.

"Are you done yet? Is Dolly all better?" Shirley kept asking throughout the procedure.

"Not yet, but almost," Rhoda Lee answered each time and kept sawing through the tough plastic.

After the arms and legs were hacked off and stored in a bag under the table, she wrapped Dolly in a tablecloth to hide the mutilated body. She instructed her sister that Dolly was sound asleep and should keep resting for the rest of the day.

Rhoda Lee snuck out and ran as fast as she could to Homer's house carrying the doll parts. She didn't hear Shirley's screaming until she was two blocks away. She would have to think up a good story to tell her mom for this one.

Everything was in place that Friday morning. The hard parts had been done in Harley's basement and in the cover of the night before. The face took some consideration. Should

Aunt Lila's dummy be smiling or scared to death? After some discussion it was decided that the real Aunt Lila Jean would be smiling at the fact that she no longer had to worry about a hit man sent by the mob.

When the fire alarm went off the next day, the school was evacuated. Mr. Dino Draggi was standing with his music class away from the school, the first period after lunch. Homer and Harley were in the class standing right next to Mr. Draggi in anticipation. Elmer was standing with his art class looking as innocent as possible after pulling the fire alarm. No one was standing next to him because stress caused Elmer to pass gas more than usual. Rhoda Lee was nowhere to be seen. Freddy said that she went home sick about an hour before. He eyed the boys suspiciously.

Homer gave Harley a slight nod. Everything was in place.

As the entire student body was facing the school there was a call from the roof. Teetering at the edge of the roof was a very strange looking woman. She was wearing a wild looking long sleeved dress that looked familiar to many who stood looking up. Her large straw hat had several ribbons flowing in the breeze and she had a purple boa wrapped around her neck.

Rhoda Lee tried to make her voice sound like a hysterical Lila Jean. "AHHHH! Life is so bad! I miss my beloved husband so much I have no reason to live!"

Homer reacted right on cue. "Aunt Lila Jean!! That's my Aunt Lila Jean!! She's going to kill herself, all because of the hit man sent by the mob!" He glanced around to see if he sounded believable.

The crowd was watching and listening intently when all of a sudden the woman on the roof jumped or fell, no one was sure. The screaming started when one of the small legs, complete with a too large, red spiked high heel, went flying through the air. It landed right next to Mary Louise Hardin who fainted... as usual. The body landed with a thud. The face that Harley had painted on the dummy smiled up oddly at Mr. Emeron.

Homer lunged at Mr. Dino Draggi screaming, as good as a fake scream could get, "It's all your fault!! She's dead!! Now you can leave this town and go back to your Mafia pals! Your cover has been blown!"

School was dismissed early. Homer and Harley were seated in front of Sister Frances and Mr. Emeron in the principal's office. Aunt Lila was sitting next to Homer. She was the one phone call he got to make. Harley dialed a wrong number and told the principal that *his* mother wasn't home. Sitting next to Harley was Mr. Dino Draggi. He had refused to sit next to Homer, as the boy was out of control. Rhoda Lee had disappeared after her Emmy performance as Aunt Lila Jean. If her Mom found out about this one she would send her to a convent to be a nun.

The boys began as usual with a lie. They made it up as they went along, something that had worked many times before.

"We are thinkin' about goin' to Hollywood and makin' movies. You keep tellin' us, Sister Frances, that we should be plannin' what we want to do when we get out of school. So ... um...." Homer began.

"So we wanted to make a movie about a saint, " Harley took over. "A lady who would not sell her soul to the devil and chose death instead and gave up her own life for her beliefs." Harley was quite pleased with his movie plot even if it did sound like a passage taken straight from the book *Lives of the Saints and Martyrs*.

Homer looked Sister Frances right in the eyes and smiled "Just like you, Sister Franken... um, Frances! Giving up a normal life so's you can teach all of us kids how to be 'Good little sons and daughters of....' "

Sister Frances wasn't buying any of it. She interrupted Homer, "She or should I say 'it' was not dressed like a lady of virtue." Sister Frances was thinking of the spiked high heels and the purple boa that had been part of the clothing on the dummy. She glanced over at Homer's Aunt Lila Jean who happened to be wearing spiked red high heels. Lila Jean saw Sister Frances looking at her shoes, pulled her feet in as far as she could under the chair, and smiled innocently.

"We were doin' a modern version," Homer said in defense.

The principal's office was very warm. Mr. Emeron stood up

and walked to the door. He opened it for ventilation and saw Elmer Whistle sitting all alone on the bench where students waited to be disciplined by the principal. Elmer took one look at Mr. Emeron and began whimpering.

"It's not my fault! They gave me a whole bunch of good food like Twinkies... and cheese curls... and those kind of buns with the white sticky icing and...."

"Elmer, I'm not quite sure what you are talking about, but I am in an important meeting. You just sit there and *relax* and I'll be with you as soon as *I* can. Remember, breathe deeply." Mr. Emeron knew that Elmer's gas problem got worse with stress and that was the last thing he needed in his small office.

Elmer hung his head. "Yes, sir, but Harley really did make me pull the fire alarm."

Elmer now had the full attention of Mr. Emeron. "What is this about, Harley?"

"I only did it to save his Aunt Lila Jean from being killed to death by Mr. Draggi."

After Elmer told the whole story to the principal, Sister Frances, Aunt Lila Jean, and Mr. Draggi, the boys had no choice but to tell the truth.

The boys explained what their intentions were, and with some reinforcement from Aunt Lila Jean, the principal and Sister Frances concluded that all in all no real harm had been done. They even admitted that the students deserved an explanation about the disappearance of their music teacher Mr. Glover, and his quick replacement, Mr. Dino Draggi.

The group listened to every word as Mr. Emeron explained. It seemed that Mr. Glover had been *very close friends* with one of the cooks, Mrs. Beckmeyer. Mr. Beckmeyer had discovered their relationship and had gone to Mr. Glover's home to discuss the matter. It ended in a rather unfortunate altercation. Mr. Glover left the hospital, and the town, the same night with a broken nose, three cracked ribs, and two black eyes.

A replacement needed to be found immediately and Mr. Draggi agreed to step in to help his old classmate, Mr. Emeron. After all, Dino owed his friend a favor, a big favor.

The boys, including Elmer, were lectured about keeping

the story confidential and jumping to conclusions. They were sent to Father Stonear for confession immediately after their apology to Mr. Draggi. The boys didn't mind confession with Father Stonear because the priest couldn't hear all that well.

Lila Jean was escorted from the meeting by Mr. Draggi. When they were both outside they broke into laughter. They both agreed that it was good to have Harley and Homer and their friends looking out for Lila Jean. Their conversation continued all the way to Mr. Draggi's car.

Dino had been born in New Jersey. His best friend throughout high school was Edward Emeron. It was Eddie who had tried to convince Dino not to go the way of his brother Rocco, who had joined the mob early. It had been perfect timing when he called his old pal Father Eddie asking if he could hide out for a while. It took thirty years for Dino Draggi to realize that his friend had been right all along. He just couldn't stomach the work of the mob. Hiding out in this two-bit town as a music teacher, with the help of his old friend Mr. Emeron, was the perfect cover.

Mr. Draggi was intrigued by Lila's fashion design. He offered to give her a ride home. Lila picked up her dressmaker's dummy that was still smiling after falling two stories and losing a plastic leg.

Mr. Draggi opened the door of his Cadillac and Lila Jean slid over on the expensive seat. She propped her dummy up next to the window requiring her to sit right next to Mr. Dino Draggi. She admired his Italian leather shoes, the luxury car and the monogrammed shirt. There on the dashboard was even the exact same St. Christopher medal that her ex-husband had on the dashboard of his Cadillac.

As a matter of fact, Mr. Draggi had a lot in common with Lila Jean's ex-husband.

"Imagine," she thought "finding a man like him in this two-bit town.

Wonders never cease.

CHAPTER SEVEN

A LASTING FEAR

Let's go fishin'," Harley said at the lunch table.

It had been a week since Harley and Homer had tried to save Aunt Lila Jean from the Mafia. Homer sort of convinced Harley that Rhoda Lee did her best to help them. She did come through with the arms and legs and had paid the price. Her mother was now convinced that Rhoda Lee was in desperate need of her attention. The brutal dismemberment of the doll belonging to her younger sister, Shirley, was a wake-up call for the mother of seven. She began checking out books from the public library with titles like *Children with Rage*, *From the Playpen to the Penitentiary*, and *Mothers Who Fail*.

Rhoda Lee now had to spend "quality time" with her mother every Saturday. It was awful.

"She says things like, 'How does that make you feel?' and 'Tell me about your fears.'" Rhoda Lee was lamenting her predicament to Homer over lunch. "I guess the worst part is that Shirley is havin' nightmares and so now she has to see a shrink. The shrink told mom that little kids don't know the difference between real and pretend. Dr. Pealer said Shirley is suffering severe trauma from watching her doll get sawed up. I think it's a crock. I'm not that psycho. After all, I did blindfold the girl."

Harley felt kind of sorry for Rodent Lee. "So, do you want to go fishin' with us?"

Rhoda Lee had a shocked look on her face. Homer was smiling. "That's a great idea."

"I don't have a fishing pole," Rhoda Lee replied sadly.

"Neither do we," said Homer.

Harley could see the confused look on Rhoda Lee's face and felt compelled to explain. "We catch catfish with our hands. My grandfather taught us. He learned it as a kid in Oklahoma. There it's called noodlin', folks around here call it hoggin'."

"We'll teach ya how ta do it," said Homer confidently.

"Meet us on Sunday after church under the bridge," Harley told Rhoda Lee.

"I'll bring ya a pair of gloves," Homer promised.

Rhoda Lee Swampson was all smiles. It had taken some work and a lot of food, but she finally felt accepted by Homer and Harley. Now she knew exactly what she would tell her mother when she asked Rhoda Lee to tell her about her worst fears. Her worst fear had always been having no friends. Now she could tell her mother that her worst fear was taken care of. Rhoda Lee could not predict that another fear would replace it. Her new fear was lying in wait under a limestone ledge in the Joachim Creek.

Rhoda Lee changed quickly after church to go for a hike. Her mother was pleased until she noticed that more food was missing. Rhoda Lee didn't seem to be putting on any extra weight. Where was all that food going?

Harley and Homer were waiting for her under the bridge. Homer handed Rhoda Lee a pair of mechanics' gloves that he had taken from his dad's secret stash. He glanced down and smiled at the large bag that Rhoda Lee had brought along.

"There are a couple a ways to noodle for catfish," Harley explained. "Grandpa's way is ta wriggle your finger to attract the attention of a catfish. You wait to feel a nip and if the fish is big enough it'll swallow your hand. Once your hand is inside of the fish you hook your thumb through a gill and use your other hand to grab it behind the head."

Rhoda Lee was amazed that Harley spoke with such knowledge. He was smarter than people thought. Harley was smart enough to know what not to tell Rhoda Lee. He left out the part about not knowing what was nipping your finger in the dark water. There were creatures that loved to live in the gumbo mud as much as catfish... snapping turtles and snakes, for example. Harley's grandfather had told him tales of noodlers with missing digits, snakebites and scars on their hands, and arms from the maxillary teeth. These teeth are pointed inward so their food cannot escape. Rhoda Lee was right. Harley was not as dumb as folks believed.

"Now the one thing ya have to remember is to be quiet. These fish can spook easy," Harley instructed.

They walked quietly along the bank of the creek, Harley leading, then Homer, with Rhoda Lee bringing up the rear. About a quarter of a mile later Harley signaled for the other two to join him a few feet from the water's edge. He began whispering the noodling instructions to Rhoda Lee.

For a girl, Rhoda Lee reacted very well. She didn't refuse to try, she didn't turn her nose up, and best of all, she didn't yell. Maybe she wasn't as bad as Harley originally thought.

Homer took his place on his belly, next to the creek, over the edge of the limestone ledge that was slightly under the surface of the water. Rhoda Lee positioned herself on her stomach next to Homer so she could watch how the noodling was done. Harley was next to Rhoda Lee. She had never seen the boys so quiet and still.

After several minutes, Rhoda Lee heard what she thought was singing. She looked at Homer quizzically. Homer whispered that just around the bend in the creek was a place where people got baptized. It was hidden by some thick sumac bushes. He wasn't sure of the religion. He had witnessed it one Sunday when Harley first taught Homer how to fish by hand. He said that the preacher dunked the folks all the way under the water.

Suddenly Harley brought his hand out of the water and there was a whiskered catfish attached. He smiled from ear to ear. That encouraged Rhoda Lee to try her hand at it. Homer told her to put on the gloves but Rhoda Lee refused. He helped guide her hand below the water and slightly under the ledge. He probably held on longer than he needed to but Rhoda Lee sure didn't mind.

* * *

The sky was blue, the day was warm, and all seemed right

for the preacher, Reverend Cletus R. Soloman. His new congregation was growing by five new members with today's baptisms. His sermons about fire and brimstone and the devil had been bringing in more folks, and the weekly contributions were increasing.

He was standing in the water of the Joachim Creek before the five new members of his congregation looking holier than Moses. He had on his new white robes holding his bible open before him. He truly believed that this was one of his best days as a preacher.

*   *   *

Rhoda Lee wasn't quite sure what the nibbling of a catfish on your finger was supposed to feel like. She did indeed feel something brushing up against her hand. If only she could catch a fish with her hand, that would surely impress Homer, even more than the food she brought along. There was really nothing to lose by grabbing the creature under the limestone ledge. Harley had made it look so easy.

*   *   *

The minister and his entire congregation, including the five new baptismal candidates, heard the scream first. They were looking around to see where it was coming from.

The snake that Rhoda Lee had grabbed and pulled from the water was a small water snake. It was not poisonous, but Rhoda Lee didn't realize that. She was smiling at Homer as she brought it out of the water. It was when she got a look at exactly what she had in her hand that she flung it up into the air with the power that comes from someone scared beyond belief. The shiny reptile flew over the tall sumac bushes and landed with a wet thud onto the open bible that the preacher was holding. This came at the exact time the preacher was warning his people about the power of the devil. Out of instinct or fear, the minister slammed the bible shut, the small water snake caught between the holy pages like a living bookmark. The sight did indeed look like a miracle.

Rhoda Lee was screaming and running as fast as she could. Harley was in hot pursuit while Homer stopped just long enough to grab the bag of food.

It was the kind of incident that can create a lasting fear in a young girl and an unforgettable moment for a congregation that watched with gaping mouths as their minister held up the bible, closed tight on the writhing snake, to prove that the holy book was indeed more powerful than the devil.

"Hallelujah, brothers and sisters!" proclaimed Reverend Cletus R. Soloman.

"AMEN!" chorused the congregation.

CHAPTER EIGHT

REVENGE IN THE FORM OF A SWEETHEART

Mrs. Swampson was more confused than ever with her daughter's behavior. She thought that she was making progress. Rhoda Lee was spending time with friends, she was becoming more concerned about her hygiene, and she was actually very receptive to her mother's weekly "quality time" get-togethers. All was going well until Rhoda Lee started having severe anxiety attacks about snakes. It all started on a Sunday afternoon in late spring.

Rhoda Lee had come home after spending time with her friends, students in her fifth grade class. She looked somewhat distraught, but Mrs. Swampson was trying to be very careful about what she said. She had read "when directly confronting an angry and possibly violent child one should remain very calm." This was hard for her to do when her daughter had used a meat cleaver to chop a black extension cord in two while she was screaming "SNAKE!!"

Homer had also noticed a change in Rhoda Lee's behavior. She was very nervous lately. She refused to use the rope swing and she went to sit at another table when Harley brought leftover spaghetti for lunch. Every time she sat down she pulled her feet off the floor and sat on them. Untied shoe strings even made her jump.

Homer wanted to undo the damage that had been caused by the fishing incident, but he wasn't sure how. He discussed it with Harley the next morning at the slide.

"My grandfather always says that when you fall off of a horse that you just have to git right back on and ride," Harley advised.

"I don't think that riding a horse is gonna help much Harley. Is that the best you can come up with?" Homer looked disappointed.

"It means that we should take her fishing again," Harley clarified.

"What the hell good is that gonna do?!" demanded Homer.

"I don't know Homer. I don't make up them sayings, I just repeat 'em. It does sound dumb don't it?" Harley said. "I think that maybe if we just try to get her mind offa snakes and onta somethin' else that it might cure her."

Harley and Homer tried everything they knew to distract Rhoda Lee every time she looked like she was thinking about snakes. They told some of Rhoda Lee's favorite chicken jokes. She'd laugh a little and then go somber again. They told stories of some of the successful pranks they'd pulled or some that failed miserably. Rhoda Lee would look down at her hand, (Homer called it her snake hand), twitch a couple of times, and bite her lip. It was a sad display for the two friends to watch.

To make matters worse, Freddy had found out about Rhoda Lee's unfortunate snake encounter and took full advantage of it. He seized every opportunity to scare Rhoda Lee even more. In science class he chose to do his report on the world's most deadly snakes.

"The most poisonous snake of all is the deadly sea snake," Freddy made his voice sound like someone from a horror movie. "It lurks in the depths of the dark water just waiting for ..."

Rhoda Lee headed for the nurse's office.

The next day Freddy pulled out all of the stops and brought a five foot black rubber snake to school. He strategically placed it in the girls' shower room. Rhoda Lee had run out in only a towel and it was flapping and flipping in such a way that students saw more of Rhoda Lee than they should have.

That particular scene put Homer over the edge. He wanted

to get back at Freddy in the worst way.

* * *

Elmer Whistle had an unusual pet. Sweetheart was a goat that was not exactly a sweetheart. The Whistle family lived on a small farm outside of town. The farm was about seven acres which doesn't sound all that small, but when you keep twelve cows, a bull, a flock of geese, a mule, various numbers of rabbits in hutches (depending on the season), four pigs, a parakeet, twenty-four speckled bantam chickens roosting in the trees, and an ornery billy goat named Sweetheart, the place did seem a tad crowded.

The Nubian goat had been a special gift to Elmer from his grandmother. She bought it when it was a very cute baby, hence the name Sweetheart. She did not realize that it would outgrow the cute name.

Elmer was teaching his pet tricks. The goat had learned to sit down quietly if it was going for a ride in Elmer's wagon. Just like dog owners know when their dogs hear the word "walk," the dogs get all excited and run for the door, Sweetheart had learned to respond to the word "ride." The horned animal would head straight for Elmer's red wagon and try to climb in.

Elmer also taught the goat to "Sit Down" and "Stay Down." Elmer had trained Sweetheart by giving him some corn mash that he had found behind the barn. What Elmer didn't realize was that the mash had fermented and what he was using to train his pet had the same alcohol content as good Kentucky whiskey. It might have been that Sweetheart could just no longer stand upright after Elmer had given him several doses of the fermented mash. That's why the goat always associated sitting with booze. He slowly became addicted.

The neighbors smiled and folks stopped to stare as Elmer would pull his pet goat in his red Radio Flyer wagon through town when going on errands for his mother. The goat would sit upright on its back haunches and look at the passing scenery through rheumy eyes. Elmer had fixed two small red balls to the end of Sweetheart's horns just in case someone upset the old goat. His pet had a reputation for butting things or people that annoyed him in any way. One thing that particularly got him going him was strong odors.

Elmer learned that the hard way when Mrs. Joleen Pillsby had walked by wearing "Summer Passion" perfume and Sweetheart took off after her in hot pursuit. Chief Davis had to rescue the poor woman from the top of the Duffner's Ice Cream delivery truck. She was screaming about how "That goat should be done away with!"

Elmer started crying.

"Aw, Elmer, don't y'all worry none about Mrs. Pillsby. She's all talk," the chief told the boy.

Elmer held Sweetheart as tears fell. The goat was licking Elmer's face, not out of compassion, the goat just liked salt, but the sight did move the chief.

"I tell ya what, Elmer, how's about I give you and your pet a ride home in my squad car," Chief Davis offered.

Elmer's face lit up. Sweetheart heard the word "ride" and butted Elmer slightly. The wagon was in the trunk and Sweetheart was in the back seat nibbling on the headrests. Elmer was up front with the friendly officer. He got to try out the lights and sirens of the squad car.

* * *

"We need to borrow your goat, Elmer," Harley looked down into the boy's eyes seriously.

Elmer knew that Harley and Homer were still holding a grudge against him for ratting them out to the principal about their attempt to get rid of the new music teacher. He had been watching his back very carefully whenever he was around them. He also had been watching how Freddy had been torturing Rhoda Lee with every kind of snake joke he could think of.

"Sweetheart ain't the kinda animal ta take ta people right off. He could hurt somebody if they wasn't careful." Elmer looked up into Harley's eyes thinking of Mrs. Pillsby.

"That's what we're countin' on," stated Harley.

Homer and Harley were also counting on Frederick Lactkey's enormous ego. He had an attitude about him that made other kids feel lowly in comparison. In other words, he thought he was hot stuff.

St. Rose School required all of the students to wear uniforms. The girls had navy blue skirts and blazers with the emblem of the school on the breast pocket. The boys were to wear dark pants, a white shirt and a tie. Freddy always seemed to wear something that made him stand out. Sometimes he wore a bow tie, sometimes pants that were pleated and had a shiny black stripe down the leg like a tuxedo. Instead of regular kid shoes, he owned shiny leather wing tips. The typical school bag that the other kids carried was not good enough for Frederick Lactkey, he carried an Italian leather briefcase.

During first period class, Freddy opened his briefcase as usual. He removed his notebook and fountain pen and placed them strategically on his desk as he did in every single class, except gym. Harley and Homer counted on his routine.

Freddy glared hostilely as Elmer "accidentally" bumped his briefcase and scrambled to pick the contents off of the floor. Harley was unusually helpful as he picked up scattered papers and placed them back into Freddy's briefcase.

The second period, Theology with Sister Frankenstein, Freddy opened his briefcase and took out his notebook. He smelled something that reminded him of Mary Louise Hardin. He would always remember the smell from the time he was sandwiched between her and Sister Germain at the May Celebration. Just the thought of being on top of Mary Louise gave him impure thoughts... even though she was not conscious at the time. He was enamored of Mary Louise. He tried every way he knew to get her attention.

That's why his heart almost stood still when he discovered a small envelope under his notebook, an envelope of pale pink that was the source of the heavenly aroma. The envelope was addressed to Frederick Lactkey, written with swirls and loops.

The envelope was one of several pieces of personalized stationery that Homer had stolen from Mary Louise's book bag.

Freddy closed his briefcase quickly and sat down. Sister Frances called the roll and Freddy was so mesmerized by the thoughts of Mary Louise that he didn't hear her.

"Frederick Alphonse Lactkey!" Sister Frances bellowed.

"Um... here... Sorry, sister," Freddy replied.

"Let us hope, Mr. Lactkey, that you will stay with us this morning as we discuss the trials and tribulations of St. Joan of Arc," Sister Frances lectured. "Or you will have some trials and tribulations of your own when it comes time for you to take the exam."

"Yes, Sister Franken ... um Frances," Freddy was still not exactly thinking about Theology.

Freddy was a different person for the next few days. His ego was still inflated and he was still not kind to people but he seemed to have lost his edge. He was in another world.

"He's not half bad when he's in love," Harley told the lunch group, making moon-eyed faces that cracked up the group. The lunch group that had begun with just Harley and Homer was expanding. It now included Rhoda Lee, Elmer and a new girl who didn't fit in with any other group, so was quickly befriended by Rhoda Lee. Eloise Polite had moved into town from an even smaller town. Her parents had taken jobs at the shoe factory. She was taller than the other girls, with curly black hair and tanned skin. Her hands were as big as baseball gloves and her feet were in direct competition. She was quiet, but when she did speak everyone listened. She hid her brains under a bushel basket to keep from being teased.

"Maybe we should call off our plan. Maybe Freddy has changed," Elmer said.

"Freddy will never change, no more than a tiger can change his spots," declared Homer.

"It's leopard," corrected Eloise quietly. "Tigers have stripes, leopards have spots."

"Tigers, leopards, whatever. I say we go right ahead with the plan. Don't forget all he did to Rhoda Lee," Homer said insistently.

"I'm just a little scared for Sweetheart. He ain't the easiest critter to handle and if he is runnin' around loose in the night he might get confused or lost," Elmer whimpered.

"We got that part all thought out. Harley found some bells to put around the old goat's neck, that way we can find him even if we can't see him." Homer was confident that the group had worked out every last detail. There were a couple of things that they didn't plan on, but then again there always were with Harley and Homer.

The love notes supposedly from Mary Louise Hardin to Freddy were more than Freddy had ever hoped for. They were short but passionate, so when a note arrived in Freddy's briefcase with the request that they meet for a secret rendezvous, Freddy was foaming at the mouth for the details. That note came when Freddy went to his last class on Friday. Freddy was to meet who he thought was his beloved Mary Louise in the garden of the rectory, where Father Stonear lived. The garden was lush with plants and bushes. The centerpiece was a statue of the Sacred Heart of Jesus which stood with open arms held out to symbolize the welcoming of everyone into the church. A small flood light aimed at the statue was the only illumination. The garden was peaceful, dark, and private. A tall iron fence covered with honeysuckle vines surrounded most of it. A large gate was kept partially open so parishioners could come in to pray. It was a perfect choice for a secret rendezvous for lovers.

Hai Karate was the name of the cologne that Freddy chose to wear. He used the whole bottle. Mary Louise hadn't given him much time to prepare, he was to meet her there that very night.

The whole gang went to watch Freddy meet his lover in the priest's garden at midnight. They had a hard time keeping quiet as they hid behind bushes to watch Freddy's reaction when Sweetheart turned out to be his date.

"Look! There he is!" whispered Homer.

"He's all dolled up and he even brought flowers!" said Harley.

"What's that smell?" asked Rhoda Lee.

"Sweetheart don't like to go out at night, so's I had to give him extra corn mash so's he'd come along with me. He was so excited that he rolled in it and now he smells like whiskey," Elmer explained. He looked at the goat that was wearing two small tiny bells around his neck on a piece of red ribbon. They made a soft tinkling sound.

"Not the goat smell," Rhoda Lee started.

"Well I am a little nervous tonight.,.." Elmer began apologizing.

"Not you either, Elmer! It's even stronger than sour mash and you put together." Rhoda Lee hissed.

"It's some macho crap that Freddy is wearing," Homer said softly, hoping Rhoda Lee didn't really like guys who wore stuff like that.

"Sweetheart has got a real good sense of smell. He's wantin' to go over there real bad." Elmer sounded strained from trying to hold onto Sweetheart.

Freddy had his back turned looking toward the gate for Mary Louise. That was a good thing. He was in a dreamlike state. He even thought he heard tiny bells. *Just like in the movies*, he thought.

The friends had all practiced sounding like Mary Louise Hardin. They concluded that Eloise's voice was the closest. Harley gave her the signal.

"Oooo, Freddy," Eloise was trying not to crack up. "I have a very big surprise for you, but you have to stay right where you are and close your eyes first."

"OK, Mary Louise, they're closed," Freddy said. He was working his lips into shape.

Harley gave Elmer the sign to let Sweetheart go. Right before the goat got to Freddy, Eloise said, "Sit down, Sweetheart."

Sweetheart sat down and so did Freddy as he responded, "Yes, Darling."

The bushes were actually quivering as the friends tried as best they could to keep from laughing. Freddy was still unaware that a goat was right behind him eagerly awaiting the chance to do what he did best, butt someone or something.

Sweetheart, the Nubian goat, was a little liquored up, inside and out. The *Hai Karate* cologne was more than he could take.

* * *

By the time Father Stonear got dressed and went out into the garden to investigate the noise, Harley, Homer, Elmer, Eloise,

Rhoda Lee, and Sweetheart were long gone.

The priest had awoken from a sound sleep. At first he didn't see Freddy in the arms of the Jesus statue, he only heard the whimpering.

The priest knew that Mr. and Mrs. Lactkey were going to be very disappointed in their son Frederick. Of course, this wasn't the first time that Father Stonear had discovered students out past their curfew. He was trying to figure out how he was going to tell those upper-class parents that he had found their son, their pride and joy, curled up in the arms of The Sacred Heart of Jesus statue, smelling of whiskey and hallucinating about a goat.

CHAPTER NINE

NEAR DEATH EXPERIENCE

St. Rose School didn't have a guidance counselor, or at least not one with a special degree in working with children and their issues. The best the school could provide was Sister Madeline Marie. Her former students called Sister Madeline Marie *Sister Mad Marie*.

Sister Madeline had come from Vienna, Austria, the same town as Dr. Sigmund Freud, the famous psychoanalyst. She was very proud of her connection to Freud and told everyone she met. She had stowed away on a boat after a disappointing engagement to a supposed Duke that lasted twelve years but ended abruptly, leaving her a spinster at the age of thirty-five.

In 1937, when she was discovered in New Jersey babbling in a foreign language, with every other word being Freud, the authorities did not know what to do with her. A religious medal around her neck was the determining factor of her fate. She was placed with an Ursuline Order of nuns. The nuns always assumed that she knew something about psychiatry because of her emotional attachment to Freud and his work. She was assigned to work with students who had emotional issues. No one ever discovered that the only experience she had working with kids was as a goat herder's daughter.

She was not a good student of the English language and didn't really care. She was transferred to Missouri when she reached sixty-five years of age. They were to be her golden retirement years. She was called back into active duty by Mr. Emeron for a very special case. A very prominent family at St.

Rose School had demanded a religious counselor for their son who had a suspected drinking problem.

Frederick Lactkey met with Mad Marie before school in her small office once a week. Freddy's pride had been bruised and he was mad at Homer and Harley and the rest of the world.

"How do you do, Fred-er-reek? I am Sister Madeline Marie. Ve vill be meeting for a vile to talk. I grew up in Vienna, the same town as the famous Dr. Sigmund Freud."

"Here we go," thought Freddy. "Just what I need right now, a crackpot old nun who wants to impress me with how great she thinks she is... just like my dad. I know so and so... I own so and so.... I AM so and so."

"Zo, Fred-er-reek, vat zeems to be za trouble?" Mad Marie looked directly at Freddy like he was a science specimen.

"I don't have any troubles, Sister. The other kids have troubles," Freddy stated arrogantly.

"I zee," the nun responded as she wrote something down in her notebook.

"Vell maybe ve can get to za bottom of your troubles." She wrote more in her notebook.

"I said I don't have any problems, Sister," Freddy said louder.

"Ve vill ze," answered the nun as she wrote.

Freddy thought that the nun was hard of hearing. "I SAID I DON'T HAVE ANY TROUBLES SISTER!" Freddy bellowed.

"Ah ... and zat zeems to make you angry." Again with the writing.

The old bat was really starting to get to Freddy. "I AM NOT ANGRY AND I DON'T HAVE ANY TROUBLES! WRITE THAT DOWN IN YOUR BOOK!" He was now red in the face as he stomped out and slammed the door.

Mad Marie made a another note in her book: "Showing resistance."

* * *

"Maybe we were a little hard on Freddy. The goat could of really hurt him," Rhoda Lee was lamenting at the lunch table.

"We left the rubber balls on his horns, didn't we!" Homer

was defensive.

"I just feel like I'm ruinin' people's lives. First Shirley is possibly damaged for life and has to see a shrink, and now Freddy." Rhoda Lee was tearing up.

"How is your sister Shirley doing?" asked Eloise.

"She won't let go of Dolly. It's sad to see her walkin' around holdin' a doll with no arms or legs. She says she will always take care of Dolly 'cuz she's handicapped."

"Does she seem sad about it?" Eloise asked.

"Not so much anymore. She acts just like a mom should. She loves that doll no matter what. I wanted to buy her a new doll but she only wants Dolly."

"Maybe she is tryin' ta be the kind of mom she wants your momma ta be. A momma who will love you no matter what." Everyone looked at Eloise as if God had spoken. She never ceased to amaze the group with her insight.

"What we all need is to go somewhere's or do somethin' ta take our minds offa everything and everybody," Harley smiled at the group.

"I have a feeling that you have somethin' in mind Harley," Homer said confidently.

"Well, there is a little adventure that I've been wantin' ta go on. I figure that we could all go." The group was all ears.

"All of us?" asked Elmer who was never invited along with other kids.

"Yeah. All of us," Harley smiled sneaking a shy peek at Eloise, looking for her approval.

In the past couple of weeks since Eloise had joined the lunch group Harley had mellowed. His mind was no longer consumed with revenge or disposing of people who annoyed him. He was even trying not to swear. The two boys had actually listened to Sister Frances talk about how it was disrespectful, especially around people you cared about. He was enjoying lunch with the group of misfits. He didn't even mind Elmer and his smell as much.

Earl Johnson, Harley's maternal grandfather, had been telling Harley stories about the old days in town. One story in particular had sparked Harley's curiosity. It was the story of a limestone cave on the other side of the Joachim Creek. The cave was where some Confederate soldiers hid during the Civil War. According to Grandpa Earl, it was used to store guns and ammunition. After a small earthquake during the war it had been sealed up by a rock slide. Grandpa Earl said that no one had ever found it.

Caves were very common in Missouri. The famous outlaws Frank and Jesse James used one to hide when the going got rough. The hidden cave that Harley and his friends were going to try to find was nestled in thick sumac bushes and poison ivy on the east side of the creek. The best way to find it would be to follow the old trail. That trail included the old swinging bridge.

Before automobiles had become popular, most folks in town walked everywhere they wanted to go. A walkway was suspended over the creek for easy access to both sides of town, east to west and west to east. It was a crude bridge made of four long pieces of rope, two were for handles that were strung from one end to the other horizontally about twenty feet above the water at the highest end points. The other two ropes were strung through steel eye hooks screwed to the ends of the boards to provide a surface to walk on. The weathered boards had about a three-inch gap between each allowing an uncomfortable, sliced view of the water below. The spaces between the boards were also just wide enough for a small foot to slip through. The rope handles and the ropes that held the boards horizontally were connected every four feet with steel rings and short vertical ropes. It was called the swinging bridge because you could hold onto both ropes of the walkway and sway back and forth. For some it was great fun, for others it was scarier than a roomful of spiders.

The group listened quietly while Harley told the story. The idea of possibly finding a cache of Civil War supplies had them hooked.

"How are we gonna find it?" asked Elmer.

"Well, my grandpa told me that a sulfur spring was close by... that's why we're bringing the goat," Harley said confidently.

"I don't like that idea," Elmer whimpered. "Sweetheart is

still acting a little strange from chasing Freddy. I think he was traumatized."

"Aren't we all," Rhoda Lee replied softly.

"Sweetheart always acts strange, but he has the nose of a bloodhound. Besides, goats are great at climbing up rocky hills. Best of all, Sweetheart can help us carry back all of the loot we find." The group was impressed with the way Harley had thought out everything so carefully.

"When do we leave?" asked Homer eagerly.

"I was thinkin' about Sunday," Harley replied.

"I can't go on Sunday," answered Rhoda Lee, "I have to baby-sit for Shirley."

"Well then we'll change it," said Homer not wanting to leave Rhoda Lee behind.

"I'll watch Shirley for you," offered Eloise.

"No" said Harley a little too quickly. He blushed. "I mean... no sense goin', at a time when we all can't go."

"I can go anytime," said Elmer eagerly. Even if they only wanted him for his goat, it was better than not being wanted at all.

"We'll just take Shirley with us," Homer beamed at the idea. He was pleased to see Rhoda Lee's face light up.

"Are you sure, Homer?" Rhoda Lee questioned.

"Yup!" confirmed Homer. No one could look at Rhoda Lee's face and object.

"Shirley will have to bring Dolly, ya know," Rhoda Lee said reluctantly.

"No problem. What problem can a handicapped doll be?" Homer asked.

* * *

Harley was in the lead. Conveniently, next came Eloise carrying a first aid kit, a compass, some rope, matches, a small flashlight, a mirror to signal for help and, of all things, a large spool of white thread.

Harley looked at her quizzically and said, "Thread? Are you plannin' on sewing somethin' on this trip?"

"I read up on explorin' caves. It's called spelunking. The thread is ta keep us from gettin' lost." Eloise smiled, knowing that she had impressed Harley.

Harley didn't have the nerve to tell her that around here all you needed was a good sharp pocket knife.

Homer walked with Rhoda Lee, who had Shirley by the hand, behind Eloise. Homer smiled as he watched Shirley gripping Dolly around the throat. She had dressed the doll as if she was going to a party, in a long sleeved, flowing dress that hid the fact that she had no arms or legs.

Rhoda Lee had packed a huge lunch for the group and it had been strapped to Sweetheart's back. The old goat hadn't liked the extra burden but allowed Elmer to have his way when given some extra corn mash. Elmer had prepared for the trip by bringing along a bag of corn mash just in case the goat got testy. The bag smelled of strong alcohol and was fastened to Elmer's belt. The goat could be led much easier that way, it would follow that bag anywhere.

The group was festive as they trooped along. When they were almost to the swinging bridge they encountered two old men who were friends of Harley's Grandpa Earl. The two fishermen stared at the odd assortment of children, one all dressed up who looked slightly odd. There was even a billy goat, equipped with two red balls on the ends of its horns, packing a large bundle.

"Howdy, Rum!" Harley nodded to the first man. Rum Washburn had a fishing pole and tackle box. He and his friend Spur Johnson had been fishing the Joachim Creek ever since they were boys. They never caught much, but they didn't mean to. Neither man could see or hear or even remember all that well. Many times they just sat on the bank and reminisced about the big ones that they had caught in their younger days. The older the two men got, the bigger the fish memories were. Harley's Grandpa Earl would go fishing with the two men on occasion, when his rheumatism wasn't acting up.

"Howdy, Harley. Goin' fishin'?" asked Rum harmlessly.

"NO! NO FISHING!" Rhoda Lee responded in a voice that was too loud. Homer gently clasped Rhoda Lee's snake hand.

"Not today, Rum. We're just out explorin'," Harley explained.

"Well it's a mighty good day to relax," said Spur looking

suspiciously at Rhoda Lee.

"Tell Earl that we say howdy." Rum ended the conversation.

Rhoda Lee was somewhat ashamed of her reaction to Rum's question. It had been several weeks since she had unknowingly grabbed the snake from under the ledge in the creek. She had always considered herself tough, not like the fluffy kind of girls that she disliked and who disliked her. Tears came more easily now. She had not given a Tinker's Dam what folks thought about her before, but now it was becoming more important. She was confused and scared. Her mother had explained it as "becoming a young lady." Rhoda Lee didn't think that she wanted to "become a young lady." Then she would look at Homer and get confused all over again.

"This bridge don't look all that safe." Elmer was good at stating the obvious.

"We've been over it thousands of times. The goat'll be fine." Harley reassured Elmer.

"It ain't the goat that I'm worried about," Elmer said softly.

"Just hold on ta both hand ropes and make sure you step right on the boards,"
Harley instructed.

"It looks awful high up off the ground," whimpered Elmer.

"Just don't look down and you won't git scared." Homer spoke with experience.

"If I don't look down then I won't know where the boards are," Elmer's voice quivered.

"I'll tell ya what, Elmer, you can tie yourself to me and that way you don't have to worry about falling," Harley offered.

Eloise pulled out the piece of rope she had brought and Harley cut a piece that he would soon discover was too short.

"What about Sweetheart?" asked Elmer.

Homer piped up, "I'll take the goat across. Just give me the bag of sour mash so's he'll follow me." Homer glanced to see Rhoda Lee with a quizzical look on her face.

"Homer? How is Shirley gonna hold on ta the rope handles if she's got a death grip on Dolly?" Rhoda Lee asked.

"Well, maybe Dolly would like ta have a goat ride?" Homer said enthusiastically while looking at Shirley.

"She's handicapped," Shirley stated.

"Well that doesn't mean she can't have fun, now does it? We'll make sure that Dolly is safe on Sweetheart's back," Eloise said in a sweet voice. She pulled out the remaining rope and helped Homer tie Dolly to the goat's back right behind the bag of food.

The parade over the old swinging bridge looked something like this:

Harley was still in the lead moving slowly because Elmer was tied to him with a too-short piece of rope. The rope was not security enough for Elmer so he was walking board-by-board with his arms fastened tightly around Harley's waist, his face buried in Harley's back so he could take a quick peek at the boards to put his feet down. He quivered each time he looked down at the Joachim Creek twenty feet below. The stress caused more gas than ever.

Eloise and Rhoda Lee had sandwiched Shirley between them. Eloise had made up a game for Shirley. She told her to always try to put her foot exactly where Eloise had just stepped. She even promised Shirley a prize when they got over the bridge if she did a good job of getting across the bridge. Rhoda Lee would be right behind her to make sure she was safe.

The kindness that Eloise displayed to her little sister got to Rhoda Lee. She had never had a friend do something so thoughtful before, except maybe Homer. She looked over the group on the old swinging bridge and considered herself very lucky indeed.

Walking several paces behind Rhoda Lee was Homer carrying the bag of corn mash to assure that Sweetheart would follow. The goat was indeed surefooted. All seemed to be going very well until the yellow jacket appeared.

Homer was a tough kid. He wasn't scared of much... except yellow jackets. He had gotten into a hive when he was playing with his Tonka trucks in his backyard when he was six. He was building a super highway when his yellow grader unearthed a nest of the swarming devils. Homer ended up with some nasty swollen stings and a nastier fear of the insects.

There is no way a person can lead a goat, hold on to a sack of corn mash, swat at a yellow jacket and hold on to two rope handles at the same time. Something has to give. In Homer's case it was the handles first. Homer let go of the handles and held on tightly to the sour mash. He was using the bag as a sort of fly swatter. The rope that was tied to Sweetheart, the Nubian goat, was released when Homer started his defense against the angry insect. The walking rope bridge began to swing as Homer attacked the bee.

Harley was almost to the end when the bridge began to rock. It was a slight movement at first, but then it started swaying like a willow tree in a thunderstorm. Harley wanted to turn around to investigate the problem but was riveted to the spot by Elmer who had Harley in such a tight squeeze around the waist that Harley was having trouble walking.

Eloise was trying to stay upright but was walking like a drunk. Shirley obediently followed in her exact footsteps giggling at the new twist of the game. Rhoda Lee had turned just in time to see Homer lunge forward to avoid the yellow jacket and let go of the sack of corn mash. It all looked like slow motion. The bag of goat goodies sailed in an arc as it went over the side of the bridge and sailed down toward the water. Elmer had been right, Sweetheart *would* follow that bag anywhere.

Lucky for Sweetheart that he was a male. His horns somehow snagged the bottom rope of the bridge and he dangled dangerously twenty feet above the Joachim creek, four legs kicking in the wind.

Unlucky for the other occupants, the goat was right about at the halfway point of the bridge. Sweetheart wasn't a huge goat, but his one hundred pounds did cause the old bridge to bow in the middle. It was sagging to such a degree that either side had sloped sharply. That was how Harley and Elmer landed on top of Rhoda Lee and Shirley and Eloise, who had toppled onto Homer. He was on the very bottom of the pile hanging over the edge looking straight into the eyes of the doomed goat. All of this weight didn't help matters at all. It made the creek closer by five feet, but fifteen feet is still a long way to fall.

In a selfless gesture, Homer reached down to try to pull up the goat by grabbing a rope, but all he managed to do was to loosen the rope that held handicapped Dolly precariously on the back of the now frantic animal.

Homer never should have screamed "Dolly!" as the large torso and head of the plastic doll dressed in party clothes fell into the creek head first. The scream not only drew Shirley's attention to what was happening, it was also loud enough to alert the two old fishermen, Rum Washburn and Spur Johnson. They had arrived just in time to see a little girl fall from the old swinging bridge into the Joachim Creek.

"Oh my God!! Spur we have ta do somethin'!!" Rum was yelling at his friend who was already taking off his waders.

Harley saw the futility of rescuing a doll when there was a good possibility that several real human beings and a goat were at the end of their rope, so to speak. He screamed down to Mr. Johnson "Let her go! We need you up here real fast!"

This confused the two old men. Why would those kids not want to help that little girl?

"Can she swim?" Spur yelled up, giving Harley the benefit of the doubt.

Shirley, who was not as panicked as Rhoda Lee would have thought, yelled down, "No. She's handicapped."

Spur looked up at Harley and then at Rum. "Bad blood... just like his daddy."

Rum nodded in agreement. "I'm goin' in after the child."

Eloise had kept her wits about her. She saw the old man struggling as he went toward deep water. She yelled "That ain't a real kid, Mister! It's just a dressed up doll!"

Eloise had an aura of credibility about her. Folks listened to her.

"Oh!" said Spur Johnson feeling slightly foolish.

Somehow the two old men came to the rescue of Sweetheart. Rum helped all of the children across the bridge. Spur hauled up Sweetheart by the horns. The large bundle of food tied to the goat had also been saved. When the entire troupe of friends was finally settled on the east side of the bridge they decided to celebrate and have lunch early. The elderly men declined Rhoda Lee's invitation to share their food. It was only ten o'clock, but it felt much later than that to the weary explorers.

Rhoda Lee had outdone herself. She had thick ham sandwiches layered with lettuce and homemade bread and butter pickles. A quart Mason jar had been filled with baked beans.

You could see the bits of onion and fatback floating inside. Slices of yellow apples had been spread with peanut butter and stuck together. Fresh gingersnaps with raisins and large pieces of gooseberry cobbler were washed down with sweet tea.

Rhoda Lee's "quality time" with her mother was now cooking together on Saturday mornings. Mrs. Swampson had read in *Bonding With Disturbed Children* that if a child displayed an attraction to something, like food, then the attraction could be used as a mechanism to bond with the child. Mrs. Swampson was not sure why Rhoda Lee had been stealing so much food but the cooking lessons were very successful. She had never felt so close to her daughter. The more Rhoda Lee associated with Homer the better her cooking got.

Everyone praised Rhoda Lee's lunch, even Sweetheart bleated his approval as he feasted on scraps and a patch of sweet blue-eyed grass. Rhoda Lee was not used to getting that kind of feedback and her eyes started to well with tears.

"You OK, Rhoda Lee?" Homer asked.

"Yeah," Rhoda Lee replied.

"Are you cryin' about Dolly?" Shirley looked up at Rhoda Lee with those big eyes.

Rhoda Lee began to cry more. "It's OK, Rhoda Lee. Dr. Pealer says that loss is natural. Everyone goes through it," said Shirley repeating what her therapist had told her.

She patted Rhoda Lee's hand. "Don't worry. Dealing with a handicapped doll can be very demanding. You just have to let things go sometimes. Dolly is in a much better place."

Rhoda Lee looked at her little sister amazed. Maybe this therapy stuff was working. She hugged Shirley even though she had peanut butter all over her.

Elmer hated to break up the touching scene but he had something on his mind.

"Harley? How are we gonna get back home?"

"Same way we got here," Harley stated.

"I don't wanna go back over the bridge. I'm... mm... scared," he whimpered.

"We can always tie you on Sweetheart's back!" said Homer smiling.

Elmer thought about the way Dolly flew through the air and landed far below into the dark water of the creek. "I vote we keep going ta find the cave," said Elmer realizing that the unknown of the future looked better than going back.

CHAPTER TEN

INSTINCTS

The near-death experience on the bridge had made the group feel more at ease. They figured that the worst was over and so good fortune must be ahead.

"Ya think that there could be any real treasure in the cave?" Homer asked Harley.

"It's hard ta know. Some folks believe that when the war was goin' on, a cave was about as good as a bank ta hide your valuables. It was safe from marauders. There were good guys and bad guys on both sides and with Missouri bein' both Union and Confederate it was hard ta tell which was which." Once again Harley had amazed his friends with his knowledge.

"Wow!" said Elmer. "Ya mean that we could find some gold or something!"

"Don't get yourself all riled up, Elmer. I think that Harley meant that anything is possible," Eloise restated.

When the sun was at its highest point the gang stopped for a rest. The group continued their fantasies about treasure.

"I'd get myself a motorcycle! And I'd buy Harley one too! We'd ride all over and race on the old back roads," Homer said dreamily. "What about you, Elmer?"

"A elephant," Elmer said so fast that everyone knew it must be something that Elmer had thought about often.

"Why an elephant?" asked Rhoda Lee.

"'Cuz I could ride it and be taller than everybody else around. When you own a elephant ya don't have ta be scared of anybody." Elmer's wish gave the group great insight into Elmer's fears. They looked at him and nodded in approval.

"How about you Rhoda Lee? What would you do with a treasure?" Homer was curious to hear what Rhoda Lee would answer.

"I guess I'd save up the money to go to college. I'd be the first Swampson ta go," Rhoda Lee answered proudly.

"I'd let you have some of my gold, Rhoda Lee, right after I bought a new party dress. Mama's gonna kill me when she finds out about my other one," Shirley chimed in. Rhoda Lee gave Shirley another hug. Homer was proud that it was his idea to bring along Rhoda Lee's little sister, even if handicapped Dolly did end up floating down the Joachim headed for the mighty Mississippi.

"Eloise... your turn," said Rhoda Lee.

"First I'd buy Homer and Harley matching motorcycles, and I'd give Rhoda Lee money to go to college. Shirley and me would go shoppin' for a new party dress, and I don't quite know where to buy an elephant but I'm sure Elmer can tell me." Eloise's list included gifts for all of her new friends and nothing for herself.

"What would you get for yourself?" asked Shirley.

But before she could answer, Rhoda Lee interrupted, "You sure have a good heart, Eloise. How did you ever end up in our group of losers?"

"You asked me to have lunch with you and you didn't even care about *who* I was," Eloise replied.

"Did I miss something?" asked Elmer.

"That's what's great about you guys. You either never noticed or else it doesn't matter none ta you." Eloise paused as if questioning herself about what she was about to tell the group. "My daddy is black and my momma is white. That makes me mixed blood." The group looked at each other after Eloise's confession. They wondered who knew and who didn't.

Homer looked right at Harley. He had been at his friend's house once when his father had been drunk and went on a rampage about colored folks.

Harley had been one of the friends who did not know. His father's words about black folks flew into his head... bad words... hateful words, some of the same words that he used to call Harley when he was drunk. Harley smiled at Eloise knowing that his father was not a good judge of character. He hadn't even approved of his own son.

"You didn't answer my question, Eloise! What do you want?" Shirley insisted.

"I'm lookin' at it Shirley." She smiled at each of her friends individually. Rhoda Lee had befriended her when she was new. Shirley held her hand and treated her just like everyone else. Homer had accepted her... any friend of Rhoda Lee's is a friend of mine. Elmer hadn't even thought about her being different. And Harley... well he was someone special. Shirley roused her from her thoughts.

"Oh, Eloise! Where's my prize you promised me for walkin' across the swinging bridge?" Shirley asked, almost forgetting Eloise's promise.

Eloise gave Shirley a big hug. "There you go!"

"That's it? I think I was hopin' for roller skates," said Shirley.

Harley was thinking that a hug from Eloise had to be the best prize in the world. "When we find the treasure Shirley we'll buy you real silver roller skates!" he said.

The whole group smiled. They were in a type of euphoria... then Elmer farted.

"Them beans were sure good, Rhoda Lee!" Elmer said, bringing them all back to the business at hand, finding the cave.

The sumac was thicker than blackstrap molasses and poison ivy crawled all underneath it. Elmer was the only one allergic to the three leaf menace that is in the same plant family as cashews. That's why they had him ride on top of Sweetheart. The goat was not only not allergic to it but tended to nibble away at it. "He's got guts of steel!" proclaimed Elmer.

Elmer partially got his wish when he was astride the Nubian goat. He sat tall in the saddle, so to speak, and had the advantage of seeing farther ahead than everyone else.

Of course for every advantage there was a disadvantage. The goat wobbled on the uneven ground causing Elmer to shift from side to side unexpectedly. Elmer gripped the horns to keep from sliding off.

Suddenly Sweetheart stuck his nose up in the air and bleated. Before Elmer could say a word, the goat took off like a shot.

"He smells it!" yelled Harley. "It's got ta be the sulfur spring!"

Everyone started chasing the goat. The path of least resistance is usually the preferable path, but not when it comes to a Nubian *billy* goat that has just had a whiff of a Nubian *nanny* goat. Absolutely nothing can stand in his way.

Elmer thought that he would be peeled right off the back of Sweetheart as the goat created his own path through all kinds of trees, bushes and weeds. The boy didn't have the nerve to look up as he was being swatted by limbs and branches continuously. His usual command of "Sweetheart sit down!" had no effect.

The goat was creating somewhat of a path for the group that was following, but it was still slow going. Every now and then they would find small pieces of Elmer's clothes snagged on a branch. If it weren't for those clues and Elmer's occasional screams of terror, they might have lost track of him.

"There's another piece of his shirt!" exclaimed Shirley who was enjoying the hunt for Elmer. She picked up a swatch of cloth that used to be a cuff on Elmer's plaid long-sleeved shirt. Shirley looked at it and wondered how it could be ripped from Elmer's arm and still be buttoned.

The group found pieces of Elmer's clothes that were as small as a peanut. On one low scrub oak branch they found the right leg of Elmer's pants.

When Elmer's screaming stopped they only had the tattered threads to follow. They were becoming increasingly worried.

Sweetheart had finally reached his destination. He came to an abrupt stop flinging Elmer over his horns. Before him stood the lovely nanny goat that he had been so hell bent to locate. Even though he hadn't seen a female goat since he had been removed from his mother and sold, his instincts took over.

Elmer wasn't quite sure what was going on. He had kept his face buried in the goat's neck as he held on for dear life. He had been poked, gouged and nearly stripped naked. Now he was flat on his back after having been flipped one hundred and eighty degrees. He opened his eyes to see Sweetheart panting and drooling overhead. He was grabbed by the foot and dragged about six feet. He decided to never open his eyes again, because it seemed that every time he did he saw something to make him panic.

Elmer listened to the animal noises in the background. He could feel the heat of the sun on his exposed skin. Slowly he moved one hand only to discover that it was still connected to his arm. He did this with all four limbs before opening one eye in a squint.

Willa Hollis watched the small boy that she had just rescued from being trampled by the goat that he had been riding. For a woman of her age, eighty-two summers, she had responded quickly to the bleating of her nanny goat, Peaches.

When Elmer finally sat up and discovered he was being watched by an old black woman dressed all in white, including a mass of white hair, he screamed, thinking that he had indeed died.

"Am I dead?" asked Elmer.

"Not today," said Willa trying not to laugh "but it sure looks like you gave it your best."

Elmer was not completely naked. He still had on one shoe, a pair of underdrawers with the important parts still attached, and a collar that was buttoned around his neck with small shredded pieces of fabric hanging down like tassels. Although he had done a good job of protecting his face, his body was covered with small cuts and abrasions.

The path that Sweetheart had left was tangled with vines, poison ivy and berry brambles, but the group persevered. They collected the remnants of Elmer's clothing so they would at least have something to give his parents. When they were near the end Sweetheart bleated, guiding them to the humble home of Willa Hollis. They were relieved to discover Elmer sitting under a small willow tree drinking an iced glass of sweet tea with a woman who at first appearances looked angelic.

Rhoda Lee ran up to Elmer and gave him a huge hug, much to Elmer's surprise. Rhoda Lee was the most relieved to see Elmer. For a while there back on the trail, she had added Elmer to her growing list of lives that she had destroyed.

"Looks like you need this," said Shirley handing Elmer the shoe that she had discovered in a patch of poison ivy.

"Wonder of wonders!" declared Willa Hollis. "What have I done to earn the visitation of such a group of children?"

"Well, Ma'am, it was your goat that got us all here," said Harley smiling. He liked Willa Hollis right from the start and he could tell that everyone else did too.

Rhoda Lee helped Willa get cold glasses of sweet tea for everyone. The elderly woman also had fresh baked lemon squares that she placed on a beautiful plate painted with honeysuckle vines. Willa placed a lemon square over a chip in the plate to conceal it. Rhoda Lee smiled. She'd have to remember to get the recipe before they left.

Willa Hollis knew even more about the history of the area than Harley's Grandpa Earl. She also seemed to know more about children.

Everyone talked freely in front of the wizened woman. They ate, laughed and discussed their adventure. Willa gave advice, but not in the lecturing way that most adults did.

"I've heard many tales about civil war caves. I cain't say as to which ones are true or not. Stories have a way of rewritin' themselves as they go from mouth to ear, ya know. As far as the sulfur springs go, I've come across a few in my wanderings here about. You children must use caution however, as them springs is warm and they have healing powers so animals congregate there. All kinds of critters. The ones we admire and the ones we're most feared of." Willa looked right at Rhoda Lee.

Rhoda Lee wondered if the old woman was a healer. She had heard about a woman on the East side of town, the colored side, who had the powers to heal all kinds of afflictions. Rhoda Lee's fear of snakes could be considered an ailment of sorts.

"How could a person go about getting' rid of a fear? A fear so powerful that it sleeps with you in your own bed?" Rhoda

Lee's question was of interest to all of the friends. Fear can be found in many beds in the dark of the night.

"First a person has ta know precisely what she is afraid of. Fear can be hidin' in many places. Sometimes it takes a different shape or meaning. Ya have to look deep and look careful when it comes to fear, sometimes the harder path is the one that's the best." Willa Hollis sighed.

"Ya mean like the devil?" asked Elmer.

"Yes, sir, Mr. Elmer. Just like the devil himself." She smiled warmly at the boy.

The sun was in the western sky. The group had a decision to make. Harley sounded determined when he brought it up.

"Mizz Willa, I aim ta find that Civil War cave. Ya got any advice on where we should turn now?" Harley looked at his friends for support.

"We've still got a fair amount of daylight left," Eloise added supportively.

"We cain't go lookin' for no treasure no more! In case you all haven't noticed, I ain't got no clothes on!" Elmer blushed.

"If all you children are determined to go find that treasure I think that I may be able to help you out." Willa smiled big enough to light a room.

Rhoda Lee and Eloise helped Willa take in the glasses and the plate. They washed the dishes as Willa went into the back part of the house. She returned with a shirt and a pair of pants. The clothes fit Elmer relatively well. Tucked in between the clothes was a small brown rag doll with many braids. It had no clothes and it had no face. Willa handed it to Shirley. "This here doll needs a friend, not a momma mind you, a friend."

Shirley hugged the doll. "Does she have a name?" Shirley asked.

"No. That there doll comes ta you with nothin', no clothes, no face, no name. What she becomes is up ta you," Ms. Hollis said wisely.

"Thank you, Mizz Willa." Shirley gave the old woman a hug.

"You are most welcome," whispered Willa Hollis.

Willa went to a small shed and brought back an old railroad lantern.

"This here lantern belonged to my dear husband Rueben, may he rest in peace. He always managed ta find his way home with this, even on the darkest nights."

"We can't take this, Mizz Willa. You might need it some night," objected Eloise.

"My Rueben is with me day and night. He takes good care of me. He would want you children to have the lantern. He was the type who believed in adventures." With moist eyes the wise old woman handed the light to Rhoda Lee. "Use this light to see exactly what you are afraid of."

Next Willa turned to Harley. She handed Harley a small stone on a thin red string. "I can see a powerful good in you, son, and I know you cain't see it right now. Wear this until you find your goodness and then pass it on to somebody who needs it more than you."

Willa continued as she put her finger on Elmer's nose. "Now Elmer, you use this here nose, the goat has a better sense of smell than you do, but Sweetheart does not have the good sense to think before he follows his nose." She tapped Elmer on the head as she said this.

As if Sweetheart could read minds, he walked over to Elmer and began to nibble on his new shirt. He was more calm than Elmer had ever seen.

"He's spent all of his energy," Willa said. "You'll have ta come again ta see if it worked. If it did indeed, I'll be namin' the baby goat Elmer. I hope y'all come back ta see it. And I expect ta read about you all in the paper when you walk inta town with that treasure."

"You couldn't keep us away!" beamed Eloise.

They all said their good-byes. As Willa hugged Elmer she tucked a small cloth bag into his pants pocket. "For the gas," she whispered.

CHAPTER ELEVEN

REST IN PEACE

Willa had rejuvenated the group physically and emotionally. They felt that they could conquer the world.

The route they chose took them through scrub brush. Harley listened for crows. When the explorers reached a place that was under limestone cliffs, crows let out caws and screeches that sounded like someone was dying. Harley explained to his friends that a group of crows was called a "murder." They now understood how someone could have come up with that term.

"My Grandpa Earl told me that if somebody is lost or hidin' in the woods that crows can help ya find 'em. He said that if you just listen and follow their calls you'll know exactly where the person is." The group listened attentively to Harley.

"Just like Mizz Willa told us," Eloise said.

"Stop." Elmer had an unusual look on his face. Sweetheart was wanting to charge ahead but Elmer held fast to the rope. "I smell somethin'," he said softly. "It smells like a box of burnt up matches."

The group stopped and to their surprise they could also smell a slightly familiar odor.

"Sulfur." Homer stated simply.

Shirley looked quizzical. She sensed something important just happened by the looks on Rhoda Lee's and Eloise's faces.

"We found the treasure?" she asked.

"Not yet Shirley, but we seem to be closer," Eloise explained.

"Good," Shirley said "'cuz my feet are gettin' tired."

Harley took the lead. "From here on we got ta look for loose rocks, rocks that look like they fell from somewhere's else. Rocks that are different colors or ones where the lines don't match up with the ones around it." Harley was not a geologist but he did listen when folks talked. He seemed to learn more that way than from books.

It seemed odd, but Shirley was the most enthusiastic about the rocks. She wanted to keep many of the unusual ones she found on the hillside. She tried to pick up a large stone embedded with tiny specks of mica that looked like diamonds. It was too heavy for her to lift so she found a large stick and tried to pry it up. The stick sunk easily into the earth for at least two feet before she realized something was odd. When the earth swallowed the entire stick she yelled for her sister.

After removing Shirley's rock and several other large boulders, the opening of the cave was visible. The group worked cooperatively lifting and moving rocks until the hole was just big enough for Harley to crawl through. Once Harley had squeezed himself through the opening, the cave became larger and sloped down. The interior was totally black. He wriggled back out and took the small flashlight that Eloise had ready for him. Once back inside, Harley crawled cautiously through a small tunnel until there was room enough to stand up. He flicked on the light. To his amazement the walls of the cave were covered with tiny sparkles of light. He took just a moment to stare at the beauty.

Homer was getting restless. He was feeling a little put out because Willa had given the lantern to Rhoda Lee. It seemed the old woman had something for everybody but him and Eloise. That seemed odd to him. You'd think that of all the children she would have given a gift to the one of her own kind, Eloise. Homer began to sense an aura of mystique about their whole day. It seemed to him that he might just wake up and discover that it was all a dream.

Homer was snapped back into reality by Harley's squeal of delight as he backed up out of the hole to the cave. Harley stood up and yelled, "Eureka!" The crows began their murderous calls.

Excitedly the group inched their way into the depths of the cave. Sweetheart bleated as he realized that he was being left behind tied to a small bush.

The mouth of the cave expanded as the group crept forward on hands and knees. After about forty feet the children were able to stand upright. Eloise asked Harley for some light as she began to unravel the spool of thread.

"Tie it to that stalagmite," advised Harley, pointing to a rock formation that stuck up from the floor of the cave like an upside down icicle. "If you tie it to a stalactite it might slip off." Harley pointed this time to a similar formation attached to the ceiling of the cave. Both formations appeared to be wet. Shirley asked Harley how come he knew so much about caves.

"My daddy took me to Merrimack Caverns when I was a kid. He taught me that the rocks that look like icicles are called stalactites 'cuz they are stuck *tight* to the ceiling. The ones growin' up from the floor are called stalagmites 'cuz they *might* reach the ceiling one day.

"Wow!" said Shirley, "Your daddy must be awful smart!"

"Not about the important things," thought Harley.

A larger room opened up in front of the group. The flashlight beam was too small to light up the expanded area.

"I think that it's time for the lantern," Rhoda Lee advised. Eloise handed Rhoda Lee the matches and a wonderful yellow light filled the room as Rhoda Lee lit it. She handed the lantern to Harley.

"No, Rhoda Lee. Willa put you in charge of that lantern for a reason. It's your turn to lead." Homer looked at Harley for approval.

"Homer's right. Willa Hollis had a reason for everything she did and said, everything from the crows to Elmer's nose. Seems ta me that she has a way of guidin' us to the treasure even when she's not here." Harley handed the old railroad lantern back to Rhoda Lee.

"You guys are scarin' me with all this spooky talk," Elmer stated anxiously. The group groaned as they smelled the gas that was a sure sign of Elmer getting stressed.

After surveying the room, Rhoda Lee had to make her first decision. There were two tunnels leading off from the main room. Rhoda Lee held the lantern up high and looked carefully into each one. The right tunnel sloped sharply downward. The fear of falling crept into Rhoda Lee's head. The left tunnel was flat and seemingly safer. Remembering Willa's advice, *"Sometimes the harder path is the one that's the best...,"* Rhoda Lee led the group to the right, holding the lantern in front of her.

The floor of the cave became slick as water was dripping from the ceiling. Rhoda Lee walked slowly and carefully as the group made their way through the cave. The thought of Eloise marking their way with thread helped Rhoda Lee's increasing fears.

Elmer was the first of the group to slip on the wet floor. He grabbed for Homer and they both went down on the slippery slope. Harley tried to help but ended up sliding with the other two boys. The entire group ended up at the bottom of the slope in a pig pile. Somewhere along the way Eloise had dropped the spool of thread.

When they had all righted themselves at the bottom, Rhoda Lee held up the lantern. They were all scared and excited at the same time. The small room they had landed in was something right out of a horror movie.

There were five skeletons all together. Two sprawled on the earthen floor wore the remnants of blue uniforms. Two more were sitting up macabrely against a wall. They seemed to be smiling under their confederate hats. The last set of bones was much larger. It lay scattered next to a small pool of water that had collected in a very large rock that reminded the children of a baptismal font.

The group approached this scene with a sense of reverence. They were very quiet as if the spell would be broken if someone spoke. Homer looked around the cave. He realized that the group of friends was quite extraordinary. There were three girls in a cave with five skeletons and none of them screamed. He didn't think he would ever have more respect for females. They were not the screaming, giddy type. They were strong, even Rhoda Lee's little sister Shirley. Homer could see in her eyes that she knew the importance of what they had discovered.

Elmer, on the other hand, grabbed Homer and held on like a tick on a hound dog. In a small voice he was the first one to speak. "Hooooly shit!"

"Elmer!" said Eloise in disbelief that he could say such a thing in the presence of the dead.

"Homer and Harley say that all the time," Elmer protested.

"Not so much anymore, and not in front of certain people." Harley gave Eloise a shy glance. "It's disrespectful to say swears when you're around people you care about."

"Sorry," said Elmer, "It's just that I never really believed that we would actually find a cave, much less a cave with dead guys in it!"

With great respect, and some reluctance, the explorers began to examine the artifacts in the cave. Homer and Harley were drawn to the remains of an old rifle that rested on the lap of one of the Confederate soldiers. The wooden stock had been damaged by the dripping water but the metal parts were still intact.

Shirley joined Eloise as she gingerly inched her way to the Union soldiers' remains. Rhoda Lee placed the lantern on a small rock ledge next to the pool of water. She wrapped her arms around her legs to hide the shivering that had started the minute she saw the first skeleton.

"This here soldier was married," Eloise was showing Shirley a small silver band on the bones of the soldier's left hand.

Elmer was fascinated by the largest set of remains. He actually picked up the skull to examine it more closely.

"Put that down, Elmer!" Rhoda Lee yelled surprising everyone in the room.

"It's OK, Rhoda Lee, this here was just a mule or donkey or something," Elmer tried to justify his actions to Rhoda Lee.

The group realized by Rhoda Lee's reaction that she was scared. Maybe more scared of this tomb than of snakes. Eloise sat down next to Rhoda Lee while Shirley joined Elmer in his attempt to reassemble the animal bones.

"There's a story here, Rhoda Lee. If only these old bones

could talk... but they can't." She put her arm around Rhoda Lee. Eloise assumed that Rhoda Lee was afraid of the obvious... the skeletons.

But Rhoda Lee's fears came from the unknown aspects of the cave, not the bones of dead soldiers. The darkness, the possibilities that were hidden in the sand, under the rocks and lurking in the murky pool of water next to her, those were the things that frightened her the most.

"Come look, Shirley! There are little salamanders living in this pool!" Eloise called to Rhoda Lee's sister.

Rhoda Lee jumped with a start and moved away from the pool. She watched carefully as Eloise fished for a salamander to show Shirley. Eloise had dipped her hand into the dark water not knowing what she might discover.

Willa Hollis' words came into Rhoda Lee's head as clear as if she were standing right next to her. *Use the light to see exactly what you are afraid of. Use the light....*

Rhoda Lee took the lantern and held it directly over the water. A clear image of herself was reflecting back. *See exactly what you are afraid of....*

Rhoda Lee studied her reflection. She realized that all of the fears were not coming from darkness, dead bodies, or creatures lurking in dark waters. She looked at her reflection and whispered, "The inside, the fear is coming from the inside. What I *imagine* is much worse than what is real." Rhoda Lee dipped her hand into the murky water.

After carefully exploring the artifacts, Harley stood up and announced, "I think it is time for us to go."

"But what about the treasure?" asked Elmer.

"If you're talkin' about gold, there ain't any." Harley looked very adult standing tall in the lantern light.

"But this stuff is antiques. We could sell it!" Elmer pleaded.

"Or we could leave it all be," Harley said firmly.

"I don't understand. You told us this was a treasure hunt. Well, we found it! Now you're tellin' us to leave it be? You sure ain't makin' no sense, Harley!" Elmer was getting agitated.

"Elmer," said Eloise calmly "Harley is sayin' that the hunt for the treasure is reward enough. You're right. WE found it!

That's worth more than a few dollars we'd get if we sold some of this stuff."

"A few dollars is better than NO dollars!" yelled Elmer.

"Look at it this way," said Rhoda Lee. "If we took the Civil War stuff out of this cave and sold it, folks would be wondering how we got it. And if we told 'em, the whole town would come swarmin' up here lookin' for more treasure."

"So what!" argued Elmer.

"These men died for what they believed in, Elmer. They deserve to rest in peace." Harley turned to leave.

"Elmer, this stuff ain't goin' anywhere... unless somebody squeals." Homer's explanation seemed to calm Elmer. "We can make sure by taking a blood oath."

Elmer didn't like the sound of "blood oath." He also didn't like the idea of leaving everything behind, but he was clearly in the minority. He had learned long ago not to go against bigger kids... at least when they were looking. With that thought he slipped something into his pocket.

Eloise found her spool of thread wedged between two small rocks on their way out.

When they got back to the stalagmite where it was fastened, she put it down next to the rock formation.

"In case we need it again," Eloise stated with finality.

Rhoda Lee put the lantern down next to the thread. "I don't need this anymore," she said with a contented smile.

They heard the bleating of Sweetheart before they saw him. He had eaten through his rope and most of the small bush that he was tied to. Elmer was amazed that he had not run off. The others in the group seemed to take it in stride considering all of the amazing things that had happened to them that day.

After the last stone was placed securely over the entrance of the cave, the friends walked toward the sunset.

CHAPTER TWELVE

HOLY SMOKE

Frederick glared at the lunch table filled with oddballs. His hatred grew as he watched the friends laugh and eat. They hadn't bothered him in days. As a matter of fact, he felt invisible. Somehow that was worse than being the brunt of their jokes.

Freddy had many reasons to hate Harley and Homer. They had humiliated him every chance they got. He always seemed to bear the brunt of their hijinks for as long as he could remember. Now they acted as if he didn't even exist. Freddy tried to control his anger but every time he looked at them he would remember times when the two boys had gotten Freddy into real trouble. For all of the things that they got by with they should burn in hell. Freddy remembered one time when they almost did.

Harley and Homer had been asked to be altar boys a couple of years back, before Homer had learned the hard way to stop playing with fire.

Homer had always been fascinated by fire. He loved to watch it and experiment with it. There was no place like a church to find fire. There were candles in front of statues that you could light for a quarter. Long wooden toothpicks were provided so you wouldn't burn your hands. Homer had discovered these by first grade. The statues were also a great source of cash, as people would put their donations in an unlocked wooden box. Homer would frequently take out *loans* from St. Joseph.

Regular Masses only required the lighting of a few candles on the altar. In the grand celebrations like Easter and

Christmas there was a lot more singing, many more candles, and an incense burner that the priest swung around on a chain. These once-a-year Masses were always very confusing for the congregation. They were never sure when to stand, when to sit, or when to kneel. Harley always thought that the nuns were at these functions sitting in the front pew so that people could watch what they did and copy them. If a nun ever messed up, nobody knew.

Homer, Harley and Freddy were asked to be altar servers at the Celebration of the Easter Mass when they were in the fourth grade. It was typical for Freddy to be chosen. He was considered the perfect student. Some people believed that he might even become a priest one day.

Homer was very excited about the prospect of having more fire than usual to be in charge of. There were extra candles to light using a long metal rod that hooked on the end. Homer imagined all of the things that he could set ablaze that were normally out of his reach. Homer called the incense burner that swung on a chain "Karate with fire." He'd feel like he was in heaven with all of those incendiary devices. Little did he know how close he would come.

Harley was very worried that he would mess something up. This was about the time that his dad got busted for violating his parole. Harley wanted his mom to be impressed. Father Stonear was very stressed during these special ceremonies. That made him rather harsh with altar boys who messed up. Sometimes the audience could hear him reprimanding an altar boy who forgot to do something, or did it at the wrong time. Harley needed Father Stonear to be in a very relaxed mood, so he felt that it was necessary to substitute the diluted altar wine with some of his dad's homemade white lightnin'. It was stronger than store-bought whiskey. He was doing it for his mother, he told Homer.

Father Stonear filled the small cut glass wine cruets before Mass. Harley knew that when the priest thought no one was looking he would take a swig before putting it back into the cabinet. Harley made it a point to watch Father Stonear before the Easter Mass. He wondered if the priest would get suspicious of the substitution. He needn't have worried though, Father Stonear knew a good whiskey when he tasted it. Glancing upward after his first swig he whispered, "Thank you, God." He took several more swigs when he thought the altar boys weren't looking. Harley sighed with relief.

It was an Easter Ceremony that was talked about for years. After it was over, people referred to Father Stonear as "Holy Smoke."

Homer positioned himself so that he was always in the right place at the right time when it came to lighting candles and the incense burner. The nuns were confused when Father Stonear called for the wine cruet early and then proceeded to drink it down. Their confusion led to the congregation kneeling, standing and sitting many more times than was required, as the nuns tried to figure out where the priest was in the ceremony. To make matters worse, it was a very warm day and the only relief was the ceiling fans.

More than anything, Homer wanted to swing the incense burner on the end of the chain. Father Stonear, who was usually selective when it came to what duties each altar boy had, could not have cared less. He wanted to get this celebration over with so he could find out where to order some more of the great tasting wine.

When the time came, Freddy stepped forward to grasp the heavy chain of the burner. Homer stuck out his foot and Freddy tripped, falling into Harley. Father Stonear handed the burner to Homer as he moved between the two to block any punches. The priest buckled, fell on one knee, and the nuns did likewise, even though they knew this was not the time to genuflect. The whole congregation followed suit.

The incense burner looked like a giant elaborate egg, decorated with beautiful metal designs. It was cut in half horizontally at the midsection, allowing the top part of the metal egg to slide up the chain. Homer held it carefully, and while the priest opened the top Homer watched him ignite the incense inside with a tapered candle that Homer was allowed to light. The breeze from the fans made it difficult. It had taken three tries.

Once the incense was fuming, along with Freddy, the wavering priest handed the whole thing to Homer. Homer lowered it to just below his knees and started to swing it gently. He looked over at Harley and smiled. The tipsy priest resumed the ceremony. Throughout various times in the mass the priest stopped and took the burner from Homer. He would then swing it back and forth while praying.

Homer was feeling more and more comfortable with his duty. He tried various swings to see which were most effective. During one of his trials, the incense burner connected with the flowing robe the priest was wearing. The robe did not immediately ignite, it just began to smoke a little.

Harley noticed first and motioned to Homer. "Psst! Homer, look!" he said as quietly as he could. Homer's eyes went wide. He wasn't sure what to do. Harley jerked his head toward Freddy. With a very quick gesture, Homer handed the burner to Freddy who was indeed taking the ceremony very seriously and was oblivious to the pending disaster.

"Here, Freddy. You better do it."

"I knew you couldn't handle it!" Freddy snipped.

It took several moments for the robe to start burning in earnest. The smell of the incense masked the burning robe and everyone thought all of the smoke was from the burner. The fire was located at the hemline of the robe so the audience couldn't see it because the priest was behind the altar by this time.

The reactions of the nuns were sincere as they again were confused by the behavior of the priest. At first he began rubbing his legs together. The nuns, unsure of what to do, stood up, with the congregation doing the same. The priest bent down, and so the nuns did too, followed by the entire congregation. It looked like a strange game of "Mother May I."

Finally, the priest , now dripping with sweat, looked down just in time to see small flames licking up his vestments.

Freddy looked down at the same time the priest did and yelled "FIRE" in the crowded church. He also grabbed the first liquid he could find. That was how the whiskey, which

Freddy thought would douse the flames, actually caused the flames to flare up just as the priest was trying to outrun the fire by going around the altar.

The nuns were so perplexed that they started to run after the priest. The whole scene reminded Homer of that children's story about the tigers running around the tree and turning to butter.

Sister Frances saved the day when she tackled the priest and proceeded to roll with him right in front of the altar to extinguish the fire.

The three church members who investigated the matter didn't find enough evidence to show foul play. They chalked the whole incident up to an over-enthusiastic altar boy practicing to be a priest.

Freddy confronted Harley and Homer but the two boys claimed ignorance. Deep inside Freddy was sure they knew the truth. Mad Marie's notebook was not thick enough to write about all of the reasons Freddy had to hate those two.

CHAPTER THIRTEEN

PAYING RESPECTS

In the sixth grade, Harley and Homer were placed in Sister Bernice's classroom. Mr. Emeron concluded that if two of the most strict nuns could not keep the boys out of trouble, perhaps giving them a teacher who was younger and more full of energy would work.

The lunch table gained an extra person that year. After everything the group had been through, they included Rhoda Lee's sister Shirley. That added up to six. There were still two empty seats, but Homer looked at them now as possible new friends. He remembered the time when Harley was the only other person at his table. He had hated the empty seats then. He saw them as just another visual reminder that the two boys had no other friends.

The noisy table was getting the reputation for having the most fun. Sister Bernice was very pleased to see that some of the students she worried most about were genuinely having good clean fun, something she had hoped Homer and Harley would find as they matured. The other students began to notice that Sister Bernice was more lenient toward the group, pretending to scold them for making too much noise, but then turning her back so they couldn't see her laugh at some of their newest chicken jokes. One time she even joined in.

"Why did the nun cross the road?" she asked the group.

The group tried to think of an answer but couldn't. Sister Bernice smiled at them and said, "Because it was a habit!"

Freddy was at a point that he was like a volcano getting ready to erupt. He fumed when he saw his arch enemies laughing and eating. He couldn't understand how such a group of losers could enjoy life so much when they had so little. The last straw was when he saw Rodent Lee Swampson offer a lemon square to Mary Louis Hardin. Mary Louise sat down at THAT table in one of the last remaining seats.

* * *

"Zo Fred-er-reek vat vould you like to talk about today," asked Sister Mad Marie.

Freddy gave her the same stone face that he had for two weeks. Mad Marie still took notes.

"Vi don't you tell me about your friends?" the nun suggested.

"Vi don't I tell you about my ex-friends!" Freddy snarled.

"Very vell then. Tell me about your ex-friend." More notes in the dreaded book.

Freddy imagined what was being written about him in that book. *Freddy has no friends.* And why is that? It's because of those two slimeballs Harley and Homer, that's why. He'd show them! And he'd show their loser freak friends, too. He would prove once and for all to this brain picking nun that there was absolutely nothing wrong with Frederick Lactkey! He couldn't wait to see the look on his dad's face when he's handed the final report that tells the world that there is *nothing wrong* with Frederick Lactkey!

* * *

Father Stonear announced the death of Mr. Bernard Duffy at the morning mass. He spoke of the kindnesses that Mr. Duffy had bestowed upon all of the parishioners of St. Rose.

The fact was that Mr. Duffy had bought his way into heaven by paying for big ticket items like a new heating system to replace the cracked boiler in the church basement. His beliefs were that he could atone for all of the sins of his past by bribing Father Stonear. He would find out in eternity that there is quite a bit of difference between bribing a priest and bribing God.

The good news for the students at St. Rose School was that classes were to be canceled for the funeral.

"Wow! A day off! This is great!" Harley whispered to

Homer. "Now we can build that fort in the oak tree next to the creek."

After Mass their plans all flew right out the window.

"Harley and Homer, I would like to speak with you." Father Stonear stood on the church steps. "I would like you to be the servers at Mr. Duffy's funeral."

"But Father..." Harley stammered.

"This is a request made by one of your teachers. You would not want to disappoint them." They were suspicious. They hadn't been asked to be altar boys since the unforgettable Easter fire fiasco.

Sister Bernice spoke to the assembly to assign their duties.

"ALL of the students are expected to attend the funeral services for Mr. Duffy. We will need a full choir to sing the Requiem Mass. Others of you will need to set up the church hall for the luncheon provided by our Daughters of Mary Society. Those of you who would like to help prepare the meal please see Sister Frances." Eloise jabbed Rhoda Lee with her elbow and smiled.

The nun continued with the assignments. "Child care workers will be under the supervision of Sister Madeline Marie." Freddy grimaced at the name. "We will also be in need of some students to clean up after the meal."

Harley and Homer's suspicions were resolved with her next statement. "Those of you who have been specifically chosen..." she stared directly at the two boys, "to be altar servers should report to Father Stonear for instruction."

"So why do ya think Sister Bernice picked us to be altar servers?" Homer asked Harley. "Do ya think that it's some kinda trick?"

"I'm not sure Homer. She has been actin' a little strange lately. Have you noticed how she's not quite so mean to us at lunch?"

"Yeah, but I think she just likes Willa's lemon squares that Rhoda Lee gives her." Homer was convinced that Rhoda Lee's cooking could solve a lot of the world's problems.

Rhoda Lee and Eloise went directly to see Sister Frances after the assembly. They were pleased when Mary Louise Hardin joined them.

"We'd like to help in the kitchen Sister Frances, if that's OK with you." Rhoda Lee spoke shyly.

Sister Frances asked "Do you know anything about cooking?"

Eloise piped up, "Rhoda Lee is a great cook, but I'm just learning."

There was only one other girl there, an eighth grader named Sophia Hampstead. When Eloise and Rhoda Lee walked in, Sophia looked strangely at Eloise and walked out. Sister Frances saw the hurt look on Eloise's face. "I'll be happy to teach you all I know." Rhoda Lee smiled to herself thinking about the mad scientist who gave Sister Frankenstein a big heart.

Elmer and Shirley signed up for Church Hall cleanup. Even though Shirley was very young, she convinced Mr. Hadler, the custodian, that doing community service was all part of her therapy with Dr. Pealer. He felt sorry for the tiny Swampson girl. He had seen her carry a pitiful plastic doll with no arms or legs. Even if he had to work two jobs he would never let a child of his be deprived of something as cheap as a new doll.

As if Freddy wasn't angry enough, he was absolutely livid when Sister Mad Marie told him of the wonderful idea she had come up with. She felt that Frederick could benefit tremendously from working with young children. Giving him some responsibility might teach him patience.

"I won't babysit for little brats!" Freddy spat out the words.

"Vat doesn't kill you vill make you strong," Sister Madeline replied.

Mr. Duffy was laid out for viewing at Underwood's Funeral Home on Main Street the night before the funeral. The group of friends all met out front at 6:30 p.m. Sister Bernice had not assigned them to go. They all went of their own accord to investigate a rumor that had been floating around town for years. They saw this viewing as the perfect opportunity to look for the mummy.

No one knew when or how the rumor started, or even if it was true. It was said that Old Mr. Underwood, the grandfather of the current Mr. Underwood, was a man of conscience. He was called one day to remove a body discovered in a boxcar by a lineman working the night shift for Missouri Pacific Railroad, or MOPAC, for short. Many men in town worked for MOPAC. Mr. Underwood had buried several who were involved in freak accidents. Reconstruction of bodies that have been in direct contact with trains called for a patient undertaker. Mr. Underwood was that man. He was well respected in town.

The body found in the boxcar was unfamiliar to the lineman, his crew, the sheriff's department and Mr. Underwood. There was a tattered wallet in the back pocket of the shiny corduroy pants that were held up by a frayed belt cinched around his waist using the last possible hole.

The wallet contained very little information and no money. A faded, cracked photo of an elderly woman smiling while standing next to a wisteria vine that crawled up the outside wall of a tiny shack gave no clues. There was no writing on the back. The only hint of the identity of the small man was a Forrestville Public Library card with the name Lester written in a child's scrawl.

The budget of the sheriff's department could not fund an investigation into the identity of the man, so Mr. Underwood was called and requested to bury the body in the Potter's Field at the back of the cemetery. Many poor souls were laid to rest there in unmarked graves.

It was the library card that did it. When Mr. Underwood saw the worn piece of paper he felt that it told a lot about Lester. Anyone who carried a library card had a special identity.

A literary man had a certain amount of class. Mr. Underwood could not bring himself to bury Lester. The undertaker knew what it would take to keep the body from decaying. He had not only studied hard for his job, he had also had a fascination with Lenin, the famous Russian leader, mummified forever for all the world to see.

So that was supposedly how the rumor started concerning the mummy in the basement of Underwood's Funeral Home. Lester had been prepared in such a way so his relatives could one day identify him and take him home to rest. Mr.

Underwood cleaned the clothes he was found in, he even polished the worn black army boots, thinking that they may be a link to identifying the man. Lester was sitting in a chair waiting, a book in his lap.

The story of the mummy piqued the boys' interest. In order to find the mummy the group had to somehow find an excuse to get to the basement. The stairway leading down from the first floor was cordoned off by a thick velvet rope with a sign that read "Employees Only."

There were three small windows near the ground on the outside of the building. Homer and Harley had tried them before, but discovered that they were locked. Someone needed to get to the basement from the inside and unlock one of those windows, that way they could come back when Underwood's Funeral Home was empty. The group decided that only one person should try it. More than that would be difficult to explain if they were caught.

Elmer and Shirley were eliminated right away because of height and Elmer's gas problem. Even though the friends had encouraged him to try Willa's cure, Elmer was reluctant. Elmer and Shirley could, however, be used as a diversion. People in mourning were very sensitive. They would be cooperative and caring, especially when it came to small children. Death oftentimes brought out the best in people.

Shirley had practiced screaming at home after school that day. When her mother asked her what was wrong Shirley smiled and said "Nothing!"

"Then why are you screaming?" asked Mrs. Swampson.

"Just for practice," answered her small daughter with a smile.

"Oh, I see," answered her mother slowly. She walked gingerly to the bookshelf where the parenting books were starting to consume the entire space. She picked up *Understanding Emotional Outbursts* and headed for the quiet of her bedroom.

Elmer's after school assignment was to eat. Beans were on the top of the list of flatulent foods he was to eat before he met the group at the funeral home. He finished his fourth helping before he dressed for the viewing.

"I've been assigned to watch the death holy cards to make sure that nobody takes too many." He smiled up at his mother as his stomach rumbled.

Mary Louise Hardin, who was very excited to be included in the group's latest adventure, was going to be a backup in case the crowd at the funeral home needed extra distraction. She had admitted to the group that her fainting skills were pretty good. She had read an article in "Hollywood Secrets" about how actresses faint on cue. She had used the trick when she wanted something from her parents and they didn't give it to her. She also fainted to get out of trouble. That bit of information had explained a lot.

Rhoda Lee and Eloise were going to be the lookouts. Rhoda Lee stayed right outside of the elegant front door of Underwood's Funeral Home. Eloise would linger at the entrance way of the large room where Mr. Duffy was laid out in a mahogany coffin surrounded by various floral arrangements.

Homer and Harley had flipped a coin to see who was going down into the basement. Homer won when the dime landed with President Roosevelt face up.

Harley would be watching the different windows outside to see which one Homer would unlock. He would then help Homer out of the window. If everything went well Eloise would hear an all clear whistle from Harley. The friends always assumed everything would go as planned.

The children filed in to pay their respects to Mr. Duffy. They weren't quite sure what to do so they watched the mourners who went before them. They waited in line quietly. They signed the guest book. They picked up holy cards with a picture of Jesus Christ on the front and Mr. Duffy's name, date of birth and death, and a prayer for eternal peace on the back. Harley's mother had lots of them. Several were used as bookmarks in the old bible that Grandpa Earl had. Harley had looked at them and wondered if they were dead relatives' cards.

Mr. Hadler watched as the children filed past the casket, each kneeling and saying a short prayer. He smiled when he noticed the little Swampson girl clutching a different doll. His smile quickly faded as he got a closer look at the doll. This one was a homemade rag doll with no face and it was made of black fabric. He wondered why in the world those parents couldn't get that child a normal doll to play with. Folks noticed the angry expression on his face and mistook it for dislike of the group of children.

"It's a good thing he never married," whispered Mrs. Gannon to her husband.

Rhoda Lee looked carefully at Mr. Duffy and wondered how he would feel if he could see himself in all that make-up. He looked very strange with lipstick, rouge and fingernails with clear shiny polish. Did everybody who died have to get done up that way? She would have to talk to the group about this.

The gold and silver banners draped across the floral arrangements caught Harley's eye, and his imagination. *"Most Precious Brother"* came from the Knights of Columbus. *"Cherished Son"* from Mrs. Duffy, the deceased's mother, who must have been one hundred years old. The one that caught Harley's eye was *"Beloved Father"*. What would they put on the flowers for a man who wasn't beloved... *"Father in Name Only"* or *"Poor Excuse for a Father"*? Would he even get flowers? Harley pulled the stone out from under his shirt and held it tightly. He could hear Willa's words in his head as the stone became warmer. He had been using it frequently lately.

Homer looked at Harley's face and knew what he was thinking. *"Beloved Father"* was not exactly a description of a father that he could relate to either.

After they paid their condolences to Mrs. Duffy and her son, Andrew, the captain of the high school football team, they met in the hall for last-minute instructions.

Mr. Arnold Scritts was doing hall duty. He was retired and liked picking up a few extra dollars by just standing in the hall and guiding folks to the right viewing room.

The main hall he was assigned to accessed not only the viewing rooms, but the smaller hallway where the bathrooms were located and the staircase that led to the basement. The distraction of Mr. Scritts was the job delegated to Elmer and Shirley. When everyone was at their assigned positions, Elmer went up to Mr. Scritts.

"Where is the bathroom?" he asked fidgeting just like Homer had shown him.

Mr. Scritts looked down at the small boy and pointed down the hall. "Why is it that kids wait till the last minute?" he thought.

Elmer walked down the hall and into the bathroom. He opened the door slightly, turned the small lock on the doorknob, and closed the door, double checking to make sure it was locked. He walked back up to Mr. Scritts and announced "The bathroom door is locked."

"Then there's someone in there. You'll just have to wait your turn," Mr. Scritts instructed Elmer.

"I don't think that I can wait," Elmer told the man and then farted. It was obvious that Elmer had prepared himself well for his mission.

"I don't suppose you can," said Mr. Scritts as he wrinkled his nose.

While Mr. Scritts was outside of the bathroom door knocking, Eloise gave Homer the go-ahead sign. Homer silently ducked under the velvet rope. As he did he knocked the "Employees Only" sign off onto the floor with a clank. He didn't stop to fix it.

Mr. Scritts returned to his post mumbling "Somebody ought ta watch what that boy eats."

He glanced around and saw the sign on the floor. Eloise worried as she saw the old man pick up the sign and look down the stairs curiously. It was time for another distraction. She motioned for Shirley. Shirley stepped up right next to Mr. Scritts and screamed.

Shirley's practicing had paid off. She let out a shriek that would take the hair off a sheepdog. Mr. Scritts reacted instantly. He knelt down in front of Shirley and tried to find out what the problem was. Shirley kept screaming until Mr. Underwood himself came out to see what on earth was going on.

Shirley was now clinging to Mr. Scritts and shoving her new doll into his face. The elderly man made out a few words in between the screams — "blind," "can't see," and "handicapped for life." He did not understand that Shirley was referring to the doll, so he held the small child closely as he inspected her eyes. He got a little too close for comfort for Shirley. She remembered all about "good touch and bad touch" that Sister Martha taught her last year. She decided that prying open someone's eyelids was definitely "bad touch"... so she kneed him in his privates. Now they were both yelling.

Mr. Underwood was watching with dismay as the confrontation between Mr. Scritts and Shirley only got worse. The funeral director noticed another child approaching and turned just in time to catch Mary Louise as she fainted right into his arms. Now both men had their hands full.

Homer, meanwhile, was opening every door he could, as quickly as he could, in search of an outside window. The rooms were all dark except for one. A very small light enabled Homer to vaguely see a small man sitting in a chair.

"Sorry. Just lookin' for the bathroom." The man did not respond as Homer hurriedly shut the door.

At the back of one dark room Homer saw the glow of streetlights outside. He moved quickly through the obstacle course of tubes, tables and embalming equipment. He let out a yelp as his shin connected with something large and metal.

He was very relieved to see Harley's face staring at him through the small window. He unlocked it and quickly scaled the wall leading to the outside. Harley whistled the all clear to Eloise. The tall girl stomped over to where Mr. Scritts and Shirley were having a screaming contest.

"What are you all doin' to that little girl?!" Eloise said in an angry voice. "Come with me Shirley honey, your momma will want to hear about this." Shirley calmly took Eloise's hand and started walking away. She turned around only long enough to stick her tongue out at Mr. Scritts who was holding himself and muttering something about "kids these days."

Mary Louise awoke from her self-induced faint. "Kindly remove your hands!" she said to Mr. Underwood as she stood up and walked away in a huff.

Mr. Scritts and Mr. Underwood looked at each other oddly and then went back to their jobs not quite knowing what had just happened.

Now that the gang had access to the basement it was just a matter of finding the perfect time. If they waited too long, someone might discover the unlocked window, or the man in the chair might get suspicious and tell Mr. Underwood about the unexpected visitor.

Even though the old man in the chair could not tell anybody anything, Mr. Underwood did talk about things with the mummy. With his cat Huxley, named after one of Mr. Underwood's favorite authors, curled up in his lap, he talked about his dislike of the job that was forced onto him through family blood. Sometimes he would light a cigar and discuss other family matters to the mummified remains. He never really discussed anything *with* Lester, but that might have been what made the dead man so valuable to Mr. Underwood ... Lester was a very good listener. Sunglasses hid the fact that the mummy had no eyes.

The large black cat also seemed to enjoy Lester. Huxley slept at the feet of the mummified remains every day. At night the cat roamed the basement of the funeral home in search of an occasional mouse or leftover bits of food. Unlike most owners, the Underwoods didn't live at the funeral home. Mrs. Underwood was a little squeamish when it came to dead bodies. One week after their wedding she declared, "I refuse to sleep under the same roof with dead people."

Homer suggested that the perfect time to investigate the basement of the funeral home would be on the night of Mr. Duffy's funeral. Rhoda Lee offered to keep an eye on "The Big Board" in front of Underwood's to make sure that no one else had died.

It was a strange custom in the small Missouri town... to advertise the dead. Large glass covered bulletin boards stood in front of each funeral home. The funeral directors then displayed the names, birth dates and the dates folks died. It was a common scene for traffic to slow down and sometimes stop in front of "The Big Boards". On hot summer nights folks would go for a ride to cool off. Many of these trips included an ice cream and a drive by "The Big Boards". Many residents found out about the death of a close relative while eating a frozen custard.

Rhoda Lee reported that there had been no new deaths since Mr. Duffy. That meant that the funeral home would be empty that night. Of course one could never be sure that someone might expire before their chance to explore the basement. It was a small town, however, and like Harley said "Most everyone will be at the funeral, the burial, and the following luncheon in the church hall. If someone drops dead today, they'll do it right in front of us."

The funeral mass went off without a glitch. The only small problem was when the priest walked around Mr. Duffy's coffin with the swinging incense burner. He held it higher than usual, remembering the Easter Fire fiasco, and hit himself in the nose. It took all the control the boys could muster not to laugh out loud.

Freddy was not at the funeral, and he was not happy. He was in a small room in the back of the church hall surrounded by the Jenkin's two year old daughter, Lilac, Rhoda Lee's two younger brothers, Sam and Griff, the three year old Sneldon twins, Rick and Nick, and one year-old Galileo Smith.

"We want to play pirates!" Sam and Griff yelled.

"I don't think that pirates is an appropriate game in a church hall," Freddy told them.

"We don't care what you say, we want to play pirates!" They were both wearing pointed cowboy boots. "If you don't let us we'll kick you!"

"Threatening me is not going to change my mind," Freddy said. He would not let himself be bullied by two small boys who happened to be closely related to Rhoda Lee.

Sam had found an old Knights of Columbus sword. He jabbed the point into Freddy's rear end as Griff kicked Freddy in the shins. Freddy relented. He would not fail at this job and give Sister Mad Marie more to write in her book.

The white staircase with rose decals that Mr. Hadler had built especially for the May Day celebration was against the back wall. Sam and Griff took turns making Rick and Nick walk the plank, the top step, while Lilac screeched and giggled every time the twins, blindfolded with Galileo's diapers, walked off the edge. Freddy watched with his head in his hands.

Eloise, Rhoda Lee and Mary Louise did not attend the funeral either. They were busy in the church kitchen making food for the crowds expected after the burial. Sister Frankenstein had taught them how to make chicken and dumplings by the gallons. The nun seemed to have an entirely different disposition in the kitchen than she had when she taught.

Ladies dropped off various pies and breads throughout the morning. Elmer and Shirley were put in charge of arranging them on two tables covered with floor-length white tablecloths.

Miss Reando brought in two pies that looked and smelled like chocolate. Elmer hid one under one of the tables. He promised Shirley that they could share it later.

Homer reported that the number of cars in the funeral procession to Calvary cemetery was at least a hundred. The whole town did indeed turn out to pay their last respects to Mr. Duffy. After they had paid those respects they all found their way to St. Rose Church Hall to fill up on the free lunch.

The girls made sure the boys got extra large portions of food when they went through the line. They sat in a corner and stuffed themselves with succulent chicken swimming in a thick gravy with fluffy square dumplings. They sopped up the gravy with warm fresh buttermilk biscuits and washed it all down with ice cold sweet tea. They strolled over to the dessert table to check out the pies. They didn't find Elmer and Shirley at their work station.

Elmer and Shirley were bored with the whole funeral thing. The long white tablecloth covering the dessert table went all the way to the floor. It made an excellent hideout. They decided to eat their pie. They were very disappointed when they tried a bite.

"Yuk! This isn't chocolate. It's prune pie!" Shirley spit out the bite into her hand.

"Well, what are we gonna do with it?" asked Elmer.

Taking a small glob, Shirley rolled it into a ball and threw it into the collection of feet in front of the table. A black wing-tipped shoe stepped on the ball. When the shoes moved on,

Elmer and Shirley could hear smacking sounds. They found the sound very amusing. They continued playing "The Shoe Pie" game, targeting red high heels, brown penny loafers and even nuns' black institutional shoes. They didn't stop until the whole mincemeat pie was gone and the floor of the church hall was more sticky than road tar in the August sun.

CHAPTER FOURTEEN

LOOKING FOR LESTER

No one else died the day of Mr. Duffy's funeral. There was a close call when Ed Boyd, who was putting goose grease on his hair while looking in the rear view mirror, broad- sided one of the cars in the funeral procession. Ms. Hilda Fronlet, the driver of the small car, was taken to the emergency room for observation and was so upset about missing the funeral that the ambulance crew feared she was having a heart attack.

Ed Boyd was ticketed for failure to yield. He was taken to the police station to sign the paperwork, but he wasn't able to grasp the pen. Folks thought that he was distraught about the possibility of causing Ms. Fronlet to suffer a heart attack. The fact was that at the time of impact of his Dodge pick-up and Ms. Fronlet's Chevrolet Nova, he unknowingly squeezed the entire open tube of hair grease and ended up with the slimy mess all over his hands and steering wheel. Every time he grabbed the pen, it slipped out and went flying. To make matters worse, he had not completed his hairdo and so his soft brown hair that was usually slicked down on his head looked like a scared porcupine. Hollywood make-up artists could not have done a better job of making Ed look like he had just seen Count Dracula himself.

Underwood Funeral Home would be empty the night of the funeral. Harley and Homer figured that it would be the perfect time to look for the mummy. After the church hall was cleaned up, the group of friends met outside to plan the night. Elmer and Shirley were still inside finishing up with the folding chairs.

"I don't think that Shirley should come. She's been through enough and if we find anything scary she might have nightmares again," Rhoda Lee explained.

"She saw all of the skeletons in the cave and she was all right," defended Homer.

"But they were dead for a while. A skeleton is not as scary as a dead body," Rhoda Lee said.

"I think that they are both scary. I agree with Rhoda Lee, Shirley is too young to go into the basement of the funeral home. There's no telling what we might find there." Eloise had a serious expression on her face. "Besides, I don't think Rhoda Lee's parents will be none too happy if they discover that Shirley is out after dark."

"Now that you mention it, I don't think that Elmer ought to go either," Harley looked at Eloise. "He gets mighty scared of things and you know what happens when he gets stressed. Besides, he lives outside of town. He'd have to walk home by himself in the dark."

"Well how are we going to tell them that we don't want them to go?" asked Eloise. "We don't want to hurt their feelings."

"Leave it to me," said Homer. "Here they come now."

"I thought that we'd *never* get out of there. Sister Frankenstein made us mop up the *whole* floor. She said that there was more pie on the tile than on the table," Elmer smiled at Shirley.

"Well we were just talking about how tired we all are and how we ought to go home and get a good night's sleep," Homer said in a singsong voice.

"Yeah," agreed Rhoda Lee. "I'm bushed."

"But what about the mummy?" Shirley inquired.

"We can do that anytime," Rhoda Lee explained.

"Besides," said Harley "He ain't goin' anywhere."

"What if someone locks the basement windows?" Shirley asked.

"And what if somebody ups and dies on us? Then the funeral home will be swarming with people?" Elmer sounded stressed, and sure enough he passed gas right then.

"Nobody is gonna die between now and tomorrow," Harley tried to sound convincing.

"How do you know?" asked Elmer.

"I'm just too tired to go anywhere tonight," Eloise stated. "So count me out."

"Me too," sighed Rhoda Lee.

"Me three," agreed Homer.

"Well, that's that,'" said Harley. "We'll meet tomorrow," Harley told the group.

Rhoda Lee walked home turning frequently to check on Shirley and Elmer who were dragging behind. Elmer waved good-bye and said too loudly "I'll see you *tomorrow* Shirley."

"Yes Elmer," Shirley said in an equally loud voice. "*Tomorrow morning* will be the next time I see you."

Rhoda Lee looked quizzically at her little sister. Shirley looked her right in the eye and smiled innocently.

When Rhoda Lee was sure that everyone was asleep she moved her pillows into the shape of a sleeping body, pulled the blanket over them, gathered the supplies she needed, and crept out of the house.

The area around the funeral home was dark. There were no names listed on "The Big Board." Eloise brought the flashlight and Homer brought a small flash camera that his grandfather had given him. Rhoda Lee brought peanut butter cookies, two rolls of lifesavers, and had stuffed her pockets with red and white pinwheel mints. She had heard that peppermint kept people alert. She figured the smell would also help. She imagined that the basement of a funeral home must smell a hundred times worse than the nurse's office.

Homer was not taking any chances. He wore a large wooden cross and two rosaries around his neck. He had even borrowed his grandfather's Knights of Columbus ring and had wrapped it with some twine so it would fit his right ring finger. That was the hand that he used to punch with. He figured that the ring would add some power, one way or the other. Harley knew he only needed Willa's stone that hung by the red thread around his neck.

The window was still unlocked when Homer offered to be in the lead. He eased it open and started to go in head first. Harley grabbed Homer's feet to lower him slowly so his head would not meet the concrete floor unexpectedly. Eloise and Rhoda Lee went next, followed by Harley. When they were all securely on their feet in the dark basement, Eloise turned on the flashlight. It cast a very dim light.

"I should've checked the batteries," Eloise lamented.

They discovered that they were in some sort of storage room. Shelves were filled with bottles of chemicals. Boxes labeled *Otis Funeral Supplies* were stacked on the floor.

"What is this?" whispered Rhoda Lee holding up a long tube connected to some sort of machine.

"Do you *really* want to know?" asked Harley.

Rhoda Lee quickly dropped the tube. It clanked to the floor. "I sure do wish I had the lantern Willa gave us."

"SHHHHHH!" warned Eloise and Homer at the same time.

The dim flashlight beam scanned the room as Eloise moved it slowly.

"This is just a supply room," Harley whispered.

Eloise shone the light on boxes marked wigs, toilet tissue, flags and yarmulkes.

They all drew an audible breath when the light beam settled on a large box labeled *Body Pouches*.

"Let's keep going before we lose our nerve," instructed Harley.

All of a sudden there was a flash of light. Rhoda Lee and Eloise let out a screech as Harley grabbed the light right out of Eloise's hand.

"Shhhh! Quit your hollerin'! It was just the flash on the camera!" Homer stated.

"What in the he...ck did you take a picture of?!" Harley asked.

"I took one of that box. The one with *Body Pouches* written on it," Homer said proudly.

"Why do you want a picture of *that*?" asked Eloise.

"You never know when it might come in handy," Homer smiled. "Like for Halloween, or to scare someone."

"Like Freddy?" asked Rhoda Lee.

"Maybe," Homer said grinning slightly.

"No more pictures," Harley looked sternly at Homer and then grinned. "Unless you warn us first."

"Where do you think Mr. Underwood would keep a mummy?" asked Rhoda Lee to no one in particular.

"Don't they have to be kept in the cold, so they don't rot?" Homer questioned.

"Actually," Eloise began "A mummy can be kept at any temperature. They only rot if there is any moisture left in the body, and if bacteria can grow."

"I read about that," Harley added. "That's why mummies can be found in hot places like Egypt, and in cold places like Siberia. The bacteria needs moisture to grow, and when they made mummies they took out all of the blood and guts."

"And the bodies that were not mummified turned into mummies 'cuz of the temperature. Bacteria can't grow if it's two hot or too cold." Eloise beamed at Harley, thinking of how smart he really was.

"So our mummy can be just about anywhere?" Homer asked.

"Yup," Harley stated.

"Then I guess we'd best keep our eyes open," Homer declared.

"I just wish we had more light. Then we could go looking in pairs," Rhoda Lee explained.

Homer had been thinking the same thing. It might not be a bad thing to be alone with Rhoda Lee in the dark. He was glad his friends couldn't see the look on his face.

* * *

Elmer had convinced Shirley that a "watchgoat" was better than no protection at all. Shirley was glad she had agreed when she saw how dark it was.

The two had decided that they would not wait to go look for the mummy. The window of opportunity was open. Unlike the older children, Elmer and Shirley did not take along any supplies. They had not anticipated any problems. The plan was very simple to them. They would go into the basement of the funeral home, find the mummy, and then surprise the group the next morning with their news.

As Eloise would say later, "Ah, the innocence of youth."

* * *

With only one dim flashlight among the four friends, it was slow going in their search. They had to stay close together and explore things with their hands when light was not available.

After the storage room, Harley directed the search into a small room that was entirely white: white tiled floors and walls, white cabinets lining the walls, a deep white sink, and a white porcelain table right in the middle that resembled an old bathtub without the sides.

Upon further inspection the light landed on a white bucket connected to the end of the porcelain table.

"I don't want to think about what this is used for," Harley whispered.

Trying to back away from the embalming table, Harley bumped into Rhoda Lee causing her to lean against the table. It swung slightly to the right and tilted downward. Rhoda Lee screamed and turned quickly, knocking the flashlight out of Harley's hand onto the tile floor. It landed with a clatter before it went out.

Everyone fell silent. Homer had grabbed Rhoda Lee's hand when he thought she was falling. Now he held on tighter. Eloise came to her senses as Harley brushed up against her. She hoped he was doing it purposely.

"We have to remember that we ARE in a place that has lights. We are in the basement. So even if we turn one on, it probably can't be seen from the outside." Eloise to the rescue. "Just look for a switch or something."

The group moved toward the walls feeling along with their hands, or as in Rhoda Lee and Homer's case, they each used one hand, not wanting to let go of each other. The walls were cool and clammy to the touch.

"Hey," said Harley, "I think I've got something. There's a chain hanging down."

No one could see the water spraying down from the emergency shower, but they all heard Harley as the cold water sprayed down on him unexpectedly.

Determined to help Harley, Eloise felt frantically along the wall for a light switch. When she clicked it on she saw Harley standing under a shower, the same kind they had in science classes in case of an emergency. Harley was still holding the chain.

It took all Homer had not to burst out laughing. Harley looked like a drowned bird. Water was dripping off of his black hair. He was soaked all the way through. Eloise looked around for something to dry him off with. She grabbed a towel next to the sink. She glanced down at it before handing it to Harley. It was covered with pink stains. She knew that blood never really washed out of anything. She threw it back into the sink disgustedly.

"I'm going back to the supply room. There has to be something in there for you to use to dry off. Come with me Rhoda Lee."

Rhoda Lee dropped Homer's hand and joined Eloise. After finding the light in the supply room, the girls found the closet that held clothing. The garments were wrapped in plastic cleaner bags so they would be clean and fresh when the owner died. The names were written on a small piece of white paper and stapled to the front.

"There aren't any men's clothes," Rhoda Lee said in a voice that Eloise interpreted as, this is a problem. "Now what do we do?"

"Harley will just have to wear something from in here so he can get warm. We'll just pick the one that makes the most sense." If anyone could get Harley into women's clothing, it was Eloise.

"What if one of these ladies dies and they find out their death dress is missing?" asked Rhoda Lee in a small voice.

"Look at the names and we'll pick the one that is the healthiest, or the youngest." Eloise started at one end of the clothes and Rhoda Lee started at the other.

"Mrs. Fleming, too old. Mrs. Wilcot, older than dirt. Ms. Spears, could die any minute. Mr. Spears... wait a minute. *Mr.* Spears name is on this pink fluffy dress. It must be a mistake." Rhoda Lee stopped her inventory and stared at Eloise.

"Maybe... and maybe not." Eloise smiled a wicked little grin that caused Rhoda Lee to erupt in laughter.

After going through almost all of the funeral clothes the girls were about to give up when Rhoda Lee discovered a plain, long white robe. It looked warm and was made of terry cloth. There was even a hood attached. "This is perfect!" Rhoda Lee exclaimed. She looked at the name tag.

"It is Ms. Reando's! She is not only pretty young, but she would understand if we had to ever explain it." Eloise grabbed the robe and ripped off the plastic bag and name tag. They even remembered to turn off the light.

The girls returned to the embalming room to find Harley trying to dry himself off with some Kleenex. He looked relieved when Eloise handed him the robe.

Homer started to go through the drawers in the cabinets that lined the walls. He was discovering all kinds of supplies needed when preparing a body, such as jaw tacks, culvarium clamps, and wound filler.

"Look at these!" He pulled out an eye shaped piece of metal. "They are 'Eyecaps!'" He placed the metal piece in his hand to show everyone. The cap was smooth on the inside but had tiny metal spikes on the outside, to hold down the eyelid.

"Grandpa said they use to use silver dollars to keep a dead person's eyes closed," Harley informed them.

"I think that was a better idea," said Eloise as she carefully fingered the spikes.

"Flash!" yelled Homer as he snapped another picture. He saw Eloise jump. "Well, you told me to warn you if I was going to take a picture."

"The warning is almost as bad as the flashbulb," Eloise rubbed her ear.

"Sorry. Next time I will say 'Pardon me, but I would like to take a photo now, if you don't object.'" The haughty tone of Homer's voice made everyone laugh, even Harley who was still dripping.

The basement was cool and Eloise could see that Harley was shivering somewhat. She suggested that he change into the robe so he could get warmer. If anyone else would have suggested that Harley wear anything that even resembled something feminine, he would have hit them. But the caring way that Eloise had said it, and the way she looked at him, he would have dressed like Queen Victoria if she wanted him to.

Harley refused to take off his wet sneakers. He did not want to step in anything you might find on the basement floor of a funeral home. He wished that he had worn his usual old black army boots, but Homer had convinced everyone to wear the quietest shoes they had.

While Harley changed, Eloise went back to the supply closet with Rhoda Lee to get a "Body Pouch" to put Harley's wet clothes in. The box guaranteed that they were water proof. Harley stuffed his wet clothes in, and pulled the hood up on the robe to warm his head.

Homer announced to the girls when they returned that he had fixed the flashlight. It worked if you just shook it a few times. He demonstrated with a shake, shake, shake.

The lights were turned out and the search continued. Homer lead the group this time, as he seemed to know a little more about the quirky flashlight than anyone else. Harley brought up the rear, the long white robe trailing behind him. There was a little more noise now that Harley's tennis shoes squished as he walked, the cellophane on the mints crackled as they were unwrapped, the flashlight needed a shake, shake, shake, and the body pouch rustled. But if the group was anything, it was determined to find the mummy.

CHAPTER FIFTEEN

CAT ATTACK, RHODA LEE'S FIRST KISS, AND HARLEY EXPOSED

One of the supplies that Elmer should have brought along was the sour mash for Sweetheart. Without it, Sweetheart was distracted by every little smell on the way to Underwood's Funeral Parlor. Elmer had a short rope around the goat's neck, but it took both him and Shirley to rein the animal in. Sweetheart pulled with all his might when they walked past the bakery. The nightly bread baking did have a heavenly smell.

When they turned the corner and faced the funeral home, Shirley thought she saw a light go out in the basement. Elmer explained to her that it was probably the reflection of the street light on the window. Shirley was a little reluctant as she held tightly to Sweetheart's rope.

The two found the window open. They looked at each other as the goat bleated. They both saw the predicament they were in. What would they do with the goat? Elmer looked around searching for a solution but there were only small bushes to tie the rope to. He remembered what happened at the cave and decided not to risk it.

Shirley looked at the window and then looked at Sweetheart. She repeated the action a couple of more times and finally said "I think he'll fit if we put him through horns first."

Elmer's eyes went wide. "Sweetheart don't do so well inside of buildings. He can get into just about everything. One time I let him in the house and he ate my grandfather's toupee... right off of his head."

"Well, can we just leave him out here bellowing?" asked Shirley. "Someone is bound to hear him."

"Oh all right... but don't say I didn't warn you." Elmer pulled Sweetheart closer to the window.

Shirley went through the window first. She landed with a thud. Elmer shoved Sweetheart's head through the window, turning it sideways so the horns could go through. One shove from the rear and Sweetheart landed next to Shirley with a surprised look on his face. He bleated once as Elmer landed next to him.

The basement was dark. Elmer whispered to Shirley, "We forgot to bring a flashlight."

"Well, it's too late now." Shirley did not want to give up so soon. She wanted to prove that she could find the mummy. Rhoda Lee and Eloise would be so surprised in the morning.

"I've got an idea." Elmer explained to Shirley that Sweetheart could find lots of things if they smelled. "I figure that if a guy has been dead a while he'll stink to high heaven. Remember that cat that got runned over in front of school and nobody took care of it for two days? It smelled so bad that Sister Frankenstein called the police chief to complain. I heard her when I was in the nurse's office getting something for my upset stomach."

"So how is that goin' to help us?" Shirley asked.

"We'll just hold on to Sweetheart's rope and let him guide us to the smell. That way we don't need any light," Elmer clarified.

"You mean like a seein' eye dog?" asked Shirley.

"Exactly," Elmer said.

There are a lot of smells in the basement of a funeral home. Everything from strong chemical odors, dead mice, and a litter box, to the remains of a tuna sandwich left in a trash can of the embalming room. Elmer obviously did not realize this. After all, the processes of death and burial are unknown to most folks, especially children.

So when Sweetheart stood up after his descent into the basement of Underwood's, his nose went berserk. Shirley and Elmer barely had enough time to grab his rope before he went on a wild run through the basement. He did not bleat, and the fact that there was no light did little or nothing to slow him down, much less stop him. He was hellbent to find the source or sources of all of those odors.

Elmer was right in one respect, Sweetheart didn't seem to need any light. The Nubian goat's only issue seemed to be which smell to follow first. The goat's olfactory sense seemed to override his brain. He took off like a bat out of hell.

The width of a goat added to the width of two children makes a small path very difficult to maneuver and doorways are impossible. Elmer and Shirley were traveling at a good clip with Sweetheart pulling with more strength than should have been possible for a goat. The two children had no idea where they were or where they were headed. They had put all of their faith in the nose of a goat. The trio was running and careening into boxes, walls and equipment that was best not seen by someone their age.

The older children were still exploring. To someone not knowing, like Shirley and Elmer, their group could be misconstrued as strange and downright scary. There was an occasional shake, shake, shake and a blink of light, there was crinkling paper, the strong smell of mint, the squishing of Harley's water-soaked shoes, and what looked to be the Grim Reaper bringing up the rear, Harley in Ms. Reando's long, white, hooded robe.

Homer stopped in front of a door when he thought he heard scratching. The whole group stopped and gathered around the door to listen.

"Something or somebody is in there," Homer whispered.

"What should we do?" Rhoda Lee whispered back.

"You take the flashlight, Eloise. Remember to shake it three short times to get it to light a little. Harley and me will open the door real slow and you shine the light in. Whatever happens... don't scream. Remember that the mummy is dead... I hope."

Homer's voice cracked at the last two words.

Huxley was very curious about what was going on outside of the door. Mr. Underwood had accidentally closed the door that evening, trapping the cat in Lester's room.

Huxley had to go in the worst way. His only means of communication was scratching. He did it to doors when he wanted in or out, and he did it to anything or anyone who happened to scare the feline, whether accidentally or on purpose.

Everything seemed to happen at once. The boys opened the door. First, Huxley screeched and attacked Homer, jumping onto his chest and digging his claws in. Homer was so frightened he forgot that he had his camera in his hand and as he fought the black cat, which he assumed was the mummy, he inadvertently kept clicking the camera causing the flash to go off repeatedly. That scared the cat more and caused him to dig his claws in further.

It seemed that the smell that most attracted Sweetheart was the mint candy in Rhoda Lee's pocket, as well as the candy that the four friends had in their mouths. So Elmer and Shirley and Sweetheart rear-ended the group as Huxley attacked from the front. All of this happened virtually in the dark. It was a scene that looked like an old movie where you could only get snatches of what was going on when either the camera flashed or the flashlight blinked. It was total chaos.

Everyone started to run. Homer ran from the cat but had a hard time because Huxley wouldn't let go. Sweetheart had knocked Rhoda Lee down and discovered the origin of the mint in her mouth. Rhoda Lee believed that it was the mummy, not the goat, that was on top of her trying to give her "The Kiss Of Death." Sweetheart was simply trying to get at the wonderful, strong smell of mint that came from Rhoda Lee's mouth. The frightened girl finally got to her feet and bolted, the goat following in hot pursuit.

The brightest thing in the hallway was Harley in the white, hooded robe. Elmer and Shirley dropped the rope around Sweetheart's neck, did an about face, and ran faster than they ever have trying to get away from "The Grim Reaper." They were too young to die.

Eloise grabbed Harley by one end of the belt on the robe, as he was running back the way they had come. This caused the robe to pull open in the front exposing a naked Harley wearing only water-soaked tennis shoes on his feet and a small stone on a red thread around his neck, but in the darkness no one saw.

Shirley and Elmer were in the lead on the way back through the maze of doorways and halls in the basement of the funeral home. Elmer noticed a small red sign that was illuminated. It read "EXIT." Without even thinking he lead the group through the door to the outside of Underwood's. The street lights provided enough vision for the group to see exactly what was going on.

Homer had finally pried Huxley, the large black cat, from his chest somewhere between the embalming room and the supply room. Once in the light Rhoda Lee collapsed and the goat went after her mint again. It was then that she realized the Kissing Mummy of Death was actually Sweetheart. Harley came into the light and the group giggled uncontrollably. He glanced down realizing that the white terry cloth robe was wide open. He quickly pulled it together and turned very red.

It could have been the relief of knowing that everyone was safe, or it could have been the sight of a naked Harley. It might have been Rhoda Lee's realization that her first kiss on the mouth was from a goat. Everything they remembered and talked about added to the hilarity. Whatever caused it, the group collapsed onto the lawn of the Underwood Funeral Home and laughed and giggled until their sides hurt.

CHAPTER SIXTEEN

SOMETHING DEVELOPS

Y ou seem to be verrry angry today Fredereek." Sister Madeline Marie sat across from Freddy, her notebook in one hand and a sharpened pencil in the other.

Freddy was curled up in his chair, his legs pulled up against his chest and his arms holding them there tightly. His hands were clasped together and the knuckles were white. "Angry" was not a strong enough word for Freddy's emotions today. He was afraid that if he said a single word, or loosened the position of his body, he would surely bound from the chair and grab Sister Mad Marie by the throat and squeeze till her wimple flew off.

He kept reliving scenes in his head of the job that had been assigned to him by this evil woman. All of those horrible little kids, screaming, running and trying to kill each other with that Knights of Columbus sword.

Mr. and Mrs. Sneldon were angry with Freddy about small scratches and bruises on Nick and Rick. The boys had explained to their loving parents that they had been made to "walk the plank... blindfolded." The Sneldon's were appalled and demanded an explanation from Sister Madeline.

Rupert and Gloria Smith also met with Sister Madeline when it was discovered that their precious Galileo's diaper had not been changed in three hours, resulting in an awful diaper rash. They also wanted reimbursement for six diapers that had been ripped and stained, "God only knows how!"

Little Lilac Jenkin missed some of the childcare activities supervised by Freddy. She simply left the back of the church hall and went outside unnoticed. Freddy was busy keeping Nick, or maybe it was Rick, quiet after he was stabbed in the arm with the sword. Freddy could not understand how so much blood could come out of such a tiny cut. It took six of Galileo's diapers to clean things up.

Lilac Jenkin was found in the alley between the church and the school playing with a questionable-looking cat that had bare spots where fur had obviously been. After learning the cost of rabies shots, Mr. and Mrs. Jenkin were also irate. Police Chief Davis was not happy either after putting out an all call alert, bringing every volunteer from three towns to look for Lilac.

Frederick's reputation hit rock bottom after that. The few friends he thought he had shied away from him, even when he tried to buy their friendship, and his group of enemies acted as though he didn't even exist. This, he decided, was worse than being their target. He felt like the Hunchback of Notre Dame, alone and ostracized.

The last straw was when Sister Madeline Marie told some of the parents of the children that he had been in charge of, that she believed Frederick was simply angry and perhaps a little unstable and she was working with him. News traveled fast, and by the next day at school EVERYONE knew that Freddy was going to Sister Mad Marie's office because he was whacked.

"Ve can only get to ze bottom of your anger Fredereek if you speak about it." The nun had her pencil poised and waiting.

Freddy was not going to give her the satisfaction. He glared at her, thinking of all of the possible ways a person could torture a nun.

* * *

"You're lookin' a little down Rhoda Lee, is something wrong?" Eloise asked across the lunch table.

"Did you hear about Freddy?" Rhoda Lee looked sadly into Eloise's eyes.

"Yeah, I guess the whole school knows by now. Sister Madeline Marie is supposed to be real good at helping people like that. I heard she even knew Sigmund Freud." Eloise hoped this news made Rhoda Lee feel better.

Homer and Harley looked at each other and shrugged at the name Sigmund Freud.

"When *will* the pictures you took get developed?" Harley was questioning Homer about the roll of film that was used when they were in the basement of Underwood's Funeral Home. Eloise and Rhoda Lee turned to listen.

"Well, it costs money to have pictures developed and right now I'm a little short on cash." Homer reached across the table and took a small sweet gherkin from Harley's lunch.

"Why don't you just borrow money again?" Harley asked covering the other pickles up with his hand.

"Who am I gonna borrow money from?" Homer crunched the tiny cucumber as he talked.

"Don't you remember your friend? You know... the one who is dead and holy?" Harley was referring to St. Joseph. Homer had told Harley that he had borrowed money from him before to help out Rhoda Lee.

Homer's eyes lit up. He gave Harley a thumbs up. It would mean another nighttime church service, and another hiding in a dark pew till everyone was gone, but he was sure he could do it again. He would take any risk to prove to everyone that the group of friends had discovered the mummy that was in the basement of the funeral home. The film was the only thing left that might give them an answer. He would steal just enough quarters from the small wooden box that was next to the candles in front of the Saint Joseph statue.

Homer was late for school the next morning because he dropped off the roll of film at FoJo Studios on Main Street to be developed. He filled out the information and paid in quarters. Miss Harkshaw took the quarters and looked suspiciously at Homer.

"It's for my Aunt Lila," Homer smiled.

Miss Harkshaw made a small "O" with her mouth. She had heard of Lila Jean, the flashy divorcee from New Jersey. She held the film gingerly wondering what could possibly be on it. The news of the new music teacher, Mr. Draggi, and Lila Jean dating had been all over town. Mr. Draggi was Italian and Lila Jean was divorced from a Mafia man, she started to imagine the kind of chemistry between two such people.

Miss Harkshaw's face turned crimson and she dropped the film on the counter.

"Are you OK, Miss Harkshaw?" Homer asked.

In a very flustered voice she replied, "This will be ready next Tuesday."

Homer headed out the door to school. His friends would be wondering why he didn't meet them before school by the slide. As badly as Harley and Homer hated school, they never missed a day intentionally... only when they were suspended. Even then, they would pack a lunch and go stay in a small clump of hydrangea bushes next to school watching through the windows, feeding small pieces of bread crusts to the birds.

Rhoda Lee, Eloise, Harley, Homer, Elmer, Shirley and Mary Louise regrouped at lunch.

Homer told them about the film and how strangely Miss Harkshaw was acting.

"I feel kind of sorry for her." Rhoda Lee passed an oatmeal cookie to Homer. "She does seem lonely. She never married, you know."

"You feel sorry for everybody lately," Shirley remarked. "Even Freddy Lactkey."

"Well nobody should feel sorry for Miss Harkshaw. She knows more about what's going on in this town than anybody else. She snoops into everbody's pictures and then spreads it all over town," Harley said without sympathy for the old spinster.

"Do you think that she'll snoop into my pictures? You think she might rat us out to Mr. Underwood after she sees the mummy?" Homer was worried.

"Chances are, Homer, that there is not a picture of *anything*, much less a mummy that we didn't even find. It was real dark and if you remember correctly you were a little wild with the camera there at the end." Eloise giggled as she thought about their crazy escapade.

When one of the group brought up one of their excursions

the whole group always ended up giggling and laughing. Sister Bernice couldn't help but smile. She remembered her years at the convent when she was a novice. The young nuns were always getting into trouble for laughing. She giggled, turned sharply and continued her cafeteria duty, but not before Rhoda Lee saw her trying to conceal her smile.

Homer was up before sunrise the next Tuesday. He was waiting at the front door of FoJo Studios at 7 a.m.

"What on earth are you doing here so early, Homer? We don't open our doors until 8 a.m. on the dot. Not a moment sooner." The middle-aged receptionist, who looked much older than her fifty-five years, fumbled in her brown leather purse for her keys.

"I was just hopin' that maybe you'd be kind enough to let me get my pictures early, with school startin' at 7:30 and all." Homer gave her one of his kindest looks, the one that worked on Miss Reando when he didn't have a pencil for class.

"Well, you're wasting your time. That roll of film you brought in hasn't got much to look at on it. Most of the pictures are so dark you can't see anything, and the couple that turned out only show legs and the head of a goat. You might as well throw your money down the toilet if you think that you're going to be a photographer," she said bitterly.

The group of friends had been right, Miss Harkshaw did indeed know about all of the citizens in the small town through their pictures. Those visual memories helped her live in a world that she had given up on... family.

"Miss Harkshaw," Homer began softly, "Can you take good pictures?"

What an odd question from the likes of Homer Hiftman. "Well... yes I can. I always wanted to go to college to be a photographer. But being poor... anyway, my parents needed to be taken care of so there was never any thought of my dreams. You have to take care of family."

"Yes Ma'am, I know what you mean." Homer looked at Miss Harkshaw and suddenly saw her in a new light. "Miss Harkshaw? Do you think that maybe sometime you could give me a pointer or two about taking good pictures?"

How long had it been since someone had needed her? Miss Harkshaw thought back to the days of her youth that sped by as she cared for her ailing parents. How many opportunities had passed for her to have her own family? These thoughts showed in her moistening eyes.

"I'm sorry, Miss Harkshaw. I didn't mean to offend you or nothin'. I know that you should be paid for lessons and all. It's just that there are some things in life that I would like to know more about, things that school doesn't teach." Homer started to turn away.

"I'd be happy to help you learn more about photography. Come on in and let's get your film. It's a good place to start." As Miss Harkshaw, the spinster, slipped the worn key into the lock of the photography studio, both she and Homer had things to look forward to.

CHAPTER SEVENTEEN

WILDEST DREAMS

The lunch table was very excited, they couldn't wait for Homer to show them the pictures. Everyone shared lunches. Eloise had made lemon squares using the recipe that Willa Hollis had given to them. It had become a tradition for the group. When something good happened or the children just wanted to celebrate, Rhoda Lee or Eloise made the magical lemon squares. They had been eating them a lot lately.

The look on Homer's face as he sat down at the table was not hopeful. He looked around, his eyes traveling from Harley's face to Eloise to Mary Louise to Shirley to Elmer and finally to Rhoda Lee. He looked into her expectant eyes last, next to his oldest friend Harley, she was the last person he ever wanted to disappoint. He clasped the envelope of developed pictures. By the way the flap was torn with ragged edges it was easy for the friends to know that it had been ripped open in a big hurry.

"Show us the pictures, Homer," Elmer said in a small voice.

"There's not much to see." Homer had lowered his eyes. "Just a lot of dark, one that I think is Sweetheart's head and a pretty good one of Harley's legs."

"Have a lemon square," offered Eloise. "We don't need proof of anything. It was one of the craziest nights of my life. It's all here in my head."

"I just wish I could have been with you. My parents are SO strict. They won't let me go anywhere!" Mary Louise said sadly.

"We'll tell you all about it," Eloise offered.

The friends began talking about the flashlight, the body pouches, Harley's shower, Sweetheart's nose, bloody towels, and with each additional memory the volume at the table rose. Everyone in the cafeteria heard the table, especially Freddy who once again had his back to the group of friends pretending not to listen.

"I think we should at least see the one of Harley's legs," Eloise said with a wicked smile.

"Might as well," said Homer, "We've seen the rest of him anyway!" He opened the envelope and started to go through the pictures. He started passing around the ones that were just shades of black. As the pictures went from friend to friend, they each thought they saw something that might be a mummy.

"Here's the one of Sweetheart's head. Look at the way his eyes are red. If we didn't know for sure that it was a goat it sure could look like the devil." Homer was down to the last photo. It was indeed a pair of legs and black army boots. He passed it to Rhoda Lee.

"Well, at least Harley and Sweetheart can prove they were there." Rhoda Lee nibbled on another lemon square.

"When do you think you took this one? It had to be before Harley took his shower," Eloise looked quizzically at the picture. Something was not quite right. "Harley, look at this carefully. Is that you?"

"Well, it is kinda dark, but I guess it is me. Look at those army boots. I'm the only one of us who wears army boots. Who else could it be?" Harley asked.

"Do you remember that we all wore quiet shoes that night? Remember that your sneakers squished as you walked after they were soaked in the emergency shower?" The look on Eloise's face was very serious.

"Yeah. This ain't me. But if it ain't me, then who the hell is it?" Harley looked around as the faces of the group changed.

"HOOOOLY SH...COW!!" exclaimed Harley. "The mummy!!"

Elmer passed gas at the revelation.

Frederick Lactkey saw the group of friends huddled together talking about something secret. It bothered him to think that those kids knew something that he didn't. He would have to leave the lunchroom before them to intercept Elmer Whistle. He knew he could make him talk one way or the other.

As he was sneaking out of the cafeteria he literally ran into Sister Mad Marie. "Ah, Fredereek. Ve have an appointment after school. Don't be late. I do believe that ve are making great progress."

"*In your wildest dreams, you crazy nun,*" Freddy thought as he quickened his pace.

Elmer was startled when Freddy opened a small storage closet door and pulled him inside. Elmer farted. Freddy realized that he should not have been so impulsive. He should have planned this for a space that had fresh air.

"What do you want, Freddy?" Elmer's voice came out as a squeak.

"Just a little information, Elmer... and I am ready to pay for it." Freddy pulled out a five dollar bill from his pocket and held it in front of Elmer. Elmer stared at the money. He had not seen a five dollar bill since his grandmother had died and the birthday cards had stopped.

"What kind of information?" asked Elmer, trying not to seem anxious.

"Your little group of loser friends has a secret, and I'd like to know what it is." Freddy waved the bill back and forth in front of Elmer's face.

"I'm not going to tell you anything, Freddy." Elmer stomped on Freddy's foot, opened the door quickly, passed gas, and then slammed it shut. He ran up the hall to catch up with his friends.

In the small dark storage closet, that smelled, Freddy realized that some things could not be bought with money. He had heard his dad talk about his workers at the shoe factory.

Sometimes he had to do things that forced his employees to do what he wanted, like when he had a special order that needed to be filled quickly. He simply told the workers that they had to work weekends to get it done. If someone refused...

he fired them.

Harley's mom, April Mae, had worked at the shoe factory owned by Mr. Frederick Lactkey IV. It was at the time when Harley's dad, Riley, first got into trouble. April Mae took off from work to go to the courthouse for her husband's hearing. The next morning she was fired. With no income she asked her father, Earl, for help. Harley's grandpa moved in with them, but only after a lot of swearing matches. April Mae was reminded daily of her terrible mistake... her marriage to Riley Hauk. Drinking until she was in an alcohol induced stupor was April Mae's way of coping. Grandpa Earl chewed tobacco and went fishing to forget about the whole mess. Harley had his own ways to try and cope.

Money meant the world to Freddy's family, but not to that group of stupid, poor lowlifes who had nothing. Frederick Lactkey the V would find another way of getting what he wanted... REVENGE.

Sister Madeline Marie waited until four-thirty for Freddy to show up for his session. She called his home, but no one answered. She knew that Mr. and Mrs. Lactkey were very important, busy people. Freddy must have forgotten. She wrote, "Freddy did not come to session, probably forgot. Will check in with him tomorrow." She closed her book, packed up her office, and locked the door.

CHAPTER EIGHTEEN

SPILLING THE BEANS

Sister Bernice had a science experiment set up after lunch. The room was very chaotic. A beaker slipped out of Rhoda Lee's wet hands, spilling some unknown liquid onto Helen Jewell that caused some smoke, which set off the fire alarm. With all that was happening, Sister Bernice did not notice that Freddy was not in class. Unfortunately, no one else noticed either.

Elmer had not been able to catch up to Harley or Homer after his confrontation with Freddy in the storage closet. He'd have to wait until the morning to tell the group about it.

No one was home at the Lactkey's when Freddy crept in silently after making a detour to the Whistle Farm. He pulled on Sweetheart's rope to get the goat into the mansion. There were twenty-two rooms, he knew exactly where to hide the goat so his parents wouldn't find it. There were rooms that no one had been in for years. He had finally figured out how to make Elmer talk.

When the phone rang at the Whistle Farm, Elmer never answered it because it was never for him. So he was surprised when his mother told him that his friend was calling and wanted to speak to him.

"Hello," Elmer said shyly.

"Hello Elmer. This is Freddy." His voice sounded cocky.

"I told you that I ain't tellin' you nothin'," Elmer looked pleadingly at his mother and she left the room.

"I know you told me that earlier, but I think that you are going to have a change of heart." Freddy was very confident that Elmer would cave in.

Elmer was almost afraid to ask, "Why?"

"How's your goat doin' Elmer? Have you checked on it today?" Freddy was having fun with this conversation.

Again Elmer asked, "Why?"

"Well, you just go check, and if you need to see me I'll meet you at the slide at school. Alone! That *is* a special meeting place, isn't it Elmer?" And then Freddy hung up. Part one accomplished.

When Elmer saw the empty pen, and the missing rope, he began to tear up. Would Freddy ever hurt Sweetheart? Then he remembered that the two had met before. That was when all of Freddy's troubles started.

Mrs. Whistle believed Elmer when he told her that he had forgotten something important at school and he had to run back to get it. He stopped only long enough to get some sourmash.

"Don't be long, Elmer. You've got stock to feed," were Mrs. Whistle's parting words. Looking back on it later, she wished she would have offered to take Elmer in the old pickup truck.

Sweetheart was nowhere to be found. Freddy was sitting on the top of the slide looking down on poor Elmer.

"Where's my goat, Freddy?" Elmer's voice cracked.

"Your goat is fine, and will stay that way, as long as you tell me what you and your gang are planning to do to me." Freddy's feet dangled over the top of the slide.

"We ain't got nothin' planned to do to you," Elmer said without conviction.

"Oh, yes you do! I can see you at that lunch table all bunched up and whispering. Everybody in school knows that you are all a bunch of troublemakers." He looked down on Elmer like he was a speck of dirt. "Now, you either tell me what's going on or your goat is history!"

Eloise always said that Elmer reminded her of the Cowardly Lion in the Wizard of Oz. Freddy scared the bejeeseus out of Elmer.

"We ain't got nothin' planned. Now you better give me back

my goat." Elmer sounded whiney.

"Not until you tell me what was going on at lunch!" Freddy was getting riled up.

"Homer was just showin' us some pictures he took. That's all." Elmer backed up a few feet as Freddy came sliding down quickly.

"Pictures of what?" Freddy demanded.

"Pictures that he took that didn't come out good because of the dark." Elmer was trying his best not to give Freddy too much information, but that's hard to do with a bully.

"Why did Homer take pictures in the dark?" He stepped closer.

"Because he couldn't turn on a light or we might get caught." Elmer knew he was in trouble the minute he said it.

"So your little gang of thieves was doing something in the dark that they didn't want to get caught at? How very interesting. Tell me more, Elmer." Freddy smiled deviously.

"No," said Elmer as he backed up again.

Freddy stepped forward and grabbed Elmer's arm. "Are you forgetting about your goat Elmer? You tell me everything and you get the goat back." He let go of Elmer's arm.

"There ain't no more to tell," Elmer said stubbornly.

This time Freddy grabbed Elmer by the front of his shirt. Elmer farted. "A little nervous, Elmer? Well you should be. Now talk or the goat...."

Sweetheart was very special to Elmer. He was sure that his friends would forgive him to save the goat.

"We went into Underwood's Funeral Home to look for the mummy. Homer took pictures so's we could prove that there really is a mummy." Elmer sighed after spilling his guts.

"And you expect me to believe that there really is a mummy in the basement of Underwood's Funeral Home? Are you trying to make a fool out of me?" Freddy was getting angry.

"Yes... I mean no... I mean yes there is a mummy and no I ain't tryin' to make a fool out of you." Elmer tried to sound convincing.

"Have you got proof?" asked Freddy.

"Yeah. Homer's got a picture of the mummy's legs and feet."

"A picture of some legs and feet aren't proof. I think that you are lying to me."

"NO! It's true." Elmer's eyes were misty. "Please give me my goat back."

"That goat of yours has to be worth a lot more than a fairy tale about a mummy. You'd better have something more valuable than that to give me... if you want the goat back alive." Freddy's eyes had turned evil.

Never had Elmer been so scared. He dug into his pocket and pulled out a button. He handed it to Freddy.

"Is this another one of your jokes? A button?" Freddy fingered the button turning it over, looking at it carefully.

"Where'd you get this?" He bent down right in front of Elmer's face.

"In the cave that we found by the crick," Elmer said in a small voice.

"What else was in the cave?" Freddy sounded like an inquisitor.

"Just some Civil War stuff, and some skeletons." Elmer sniffed, thinking of the promise never to tell anyone.

"Where is this cave?" Freddy tightened his grip.

"I cain't tell you 'cuz we made a promise that we would leave them dead soldiers alone." Elmer's voice was shaking.

"*You* made a promise. *I* didn't make a promise to anyone." Freddy smiled at the thought of raiding the secret cave of Harley and Homer and his band of weirdos. He slipped the button into his pocket, or so he thought.

CHAPTER NINETEEN

A POWERFUL GOOD

Mrs. Whistle began to worry about 5:15 p.m. Elmer loved feeding all of the animals and he knew how important it was to keep them on a regular feeding schedule.

He would never forget, especially his goat Sweetheart. His mother put the food on simmer, climbed into the old pickup truck, and headed for the school.

* * *

Sweetheart was glad to see Elmer. He had not taken a liking to Freddy. The feeling was mutual. Elmer felt drained after his ordeal with Freddy. Now all he wanted was to get his pet goat and go home. He had animals that needed feeding.

Elmer was not only cowardly, he was also gullible. He actually believed Freddy when he said that he could take his goat home, right after he drew Freddy a map that would lead to the treasure. Elmer should have known better.

It was getting dark. In Freddy's desire to get back at Homer and Harley, he did not take time of day into consideration. Finding a cave at night was going to be difficult. And now that he had Elmer and Sweetheart, he could not risk letting them go home and having Elmer spill the beans. Elmer might be scared, but he would tell everything he knew at the drop of a hat.

Desperate people take desperate measures. Without thinking of the legal ramifications, Freddy decided that he could not let Elmer out of his sight until after he looted the Civil War cave. He led Elmer and Sweetheart down into the old wine cellar in the basement of the mansion and locked them in.

Chief Davis got a call at about six o'clock that evening. Mrs. Whistle had looked all around the school for Elmer without success. She went back to the farm to get Mr. Whistle who had taken on the evening feeding of the animals. She explained Elmer's strange disappearance after a phone call. Mr. Whistle told her something else was strange, Sweetheart the goat was missing, but she was sure that he had not taken the goat with him.

The police chief did not want to repeat the episode of calling in a full alert after the last one when Little Lilac was discovered within the same block. He suggested that the Whistles continue to drive the route that Elmer would have taken to get to the school. Chief Davis was going to check with Elmer's friends to see which one had called him. He started with the Swampson girl.

Mrs. Swampson gasped as she saw the police car pull up. She figured either somebody died, or somebody was in trouble. She glanced over at her large family sitting at the kitchen table in mismatched chairs before she went to answer the door.

"Evening, Mizz Swampson. Is Rhoda Lee at home?" The seriousness of his voice frightened the mother of seven. She had been trying so hard. Rhoda Lee was spending time with her every Saturday and her cooking skills outdid her mother's. After the pirate fiasco at church, the two younger boys, Sam and Griff, had joined Shirley in her therapy sessions, as was strongly suggested by Sister Madeline. The overwrought mother of seven thought everything was going pretty well.

Rhoda Lee looked up startled. "Evening Rhoda Lee. Do you happen ta know the whereabouts of Elmer Whistle?" the chief asked.

"He didn't do anything wrong." Rhoda Lee had been hanging around with Harley and Homer long enough that she knew what to say, or she thought she knew.

"I didn't say he did. It seems that someone called Elmer at home. After that call, Elmer hightailed it to the school. His folks are worried 'cuz he didn't come home. His goat is missing too." The police officer watched Rhoda Lee's eyes, hoping to get a clue.

"The last I saw of Elmer was at lunch. He's in a different grade than me, so I don't see him that much. How about you, Shirley? Did you and Elmer walk together after school?" Rhoda Lee sounded worried.

"Nope, we had a fire drill, remember?" Shirley had catsup on her chin.

"Elmer never misses going home after school 'cuz he has to feed all of the animals. He'd never miss that." Rhoda Lee looked again at Shirley. "Do you know of anybody who would call Elmer Whistle at home Shirley?"

"Elmer ain't got that many friends. Maybe it was a teacher." Shirley looked up at police chief Davis.

"Sorry to bother y'all. If you happen ta see Elmer or hear from him, please call the station."

Rhoda Lee dropped her fork too loudly and stood up. "I gotta go look Mom. Elmer doesn't like the dark and he would never neglect his animals," Rhoda Lee said pleadingly.

"It's late and dark Rhoda Lee." Mrs. Swampson saw her daughter's eyes fall. "I'd better drive you."

Rhoda Lee quickly called Homer and Eloise. Homer called Harley. They would all meet at the school in the usual place.

* * *

It was a very long night for Elmer and Sweetheart, locked away in the wine cellar. Mrs. Claudia Lactkey came home about eleven p.m. and checked on Freddy. He was sound asleep. Mr. Lactkey arrived at about midnight and fell into bed. The last words he heard that night were something his wife was saying about getting the furnace in the basement checked because it was making funny knocking noises.

* * *

The group of friends, Mrs. Swampson, Police Chief Davis, and Mr. and Mrs. Whistle were sitting in the police station, which by then had become a command post. Sisters Frances, Bernice, and Germain had joined Father Stonear in the church for a prayer service that lasted all night.

Harley's Grandpa Earl had called out all of the Veterans, including Rum Washburn and Spur Johnson. They took to patrolling the streets in their old uniforms, or at least the parts of the uniforms that still fit.

Homer's Aunt Lila Jean and his music teacher Mr. Draggi were cruising the back roads of town. For being relatively new to the area, it was odd that they both knew all of the dirt roads in the county.

* * *

Freddy managed to get out of the house very early after releasing Elmer and Sweetheart from the wine cellar. He gave them some food and then convinced Elmer to help him find the cave by telling him that they would make a lot of money. Elmer was tired, scared, and confused. Why hadn't Harley and Homer let them carry out all of the loot from the cave the first time? He wouldn't be in this mess with Freddy if his friends had only listened to him.

* * *

The next morning there was still no sign of Elmer or his goat. The teachers decided that it was best if all of the children attended classes as usual and leave the investigating to the police department. That was fine for most of the students, but it did not set well with Elmer's group of friends.

Rhoda Lee, Eloise, Shirley, Homer, and Harley met at recess at their usual place, the slide. The group had never looked worse. None of them had slept all night and they were very worried.

As they were discussing what they could do, Homer kicked the soft dirt at the bottom of the slide. He saw a flash of metal, leaned over and picked up an unusual button.

He was turning it over in his hand. It was stamped ARK.

"That's the same button we saw on some of the skeletons in the cave," said Shirley.

"That's right!" Eloise exclaimed. "I remember Shirley asking me about the "ARK." I had to explain about Arkansas being confederate and some of the soldiers from there fought here in Missouri."

Sister Madeline Marie had a frantic look on her face as she raced up to the group and interrupted the discussion. "Fredereek is missing! Have you seen him?"

"No, sister." Homer looked at her oddly. Didn't she realize

that they were all worried about their friend Elmer?

Some people are better at putting two and two together than others. The friends had a hard enough time thinking clearly after a sleepless night. It was Eloise who looked up suddenly and uttered a single word "Cave."

The friends looked at each other. "Oh my God!" whispered Rhoda Lee. Realizing that the nun was listening she quickly said "I meant that as a prayer Sister Madeline."

"We've got to hurry! No telling what Freddy might do!" Homer yelled.

"Or what Sweetheart might do to Freddy!" Harley added.

"Do you believe that Fredereek might be in danger?" asked the nun guiltily. "I deed not know that Fredereek had a sveetheart that might vant to do him harm."

Harley looked around quickly for answers. He spied the small yellow school bus that was there to take the first graders on a field trip to the local potato chip factory. He then looked Sister Mad Marie right in the eye. "Can you drive sister?"

"It has been a vile, but I do believe dat I could manage." The small nun answered Harley in a mischievous voice.

"Stay here Shirley and call Chief Davis. Tell him where we're going," Rhoda Lee instructed her little sister.

With Sister Mad Marie behind the steering wheel of the school bus, the group yelled directions to her and told her to "step on it."

* * *

Freddy had literally dragged Sweetheart across the swinging bridge. He threatened to throw the goat over if Elmer didn't cooperate. It was a long struggle for the three to reach the entrance to the cave. They were all tired, sweaty, and not thinking as clearly as they could have been. After locating the right pile of rocks, and opening the entrance to the cave, Elmer tied Sweetheart to a bush with a knot that he knew would not hold.

* * *

Parking a bus next to a creek is not an easy task. The banks slope downward and are made of sand and soft mud. The side of the bus with the door ended up in three feet of water.

"Eees everyone fine?" asked the flustered nun.

"We're all OK, sister, but we'll have to use a window to get out." Harley hadn't realized exactly how long it had been since Sister Madeline had driven. As he was trying to pull her through the bus window, while Rhoda Lee pushed from behind, the nun admitted that it had been forty years.

Without the burdens of a goat, a handicapped doll, and a frightened, farting boy, the swinging bridge did not seem so bad to cross this time. There was one point where the wind whipped up under Sister Mad Marie's habit and for a second she looked a great deal like a black hot air balloon, but that was the only dramatic part of the crossing.

Not far behind was Police Chief Davis driving his cruiser with the lights flashing and the sirens wailing. Shirley was in the front seat and Sisters Germain and Bernice were in the back begging Shirley to take it easy with the siren. They stopped abruptly when they saw the school bus partly submerged in the Joachim Creek. Shirley led the way to the swinging bridge.

* * *

Aunt Lila Jean and Mr. Draggi had stopped just long enough to pick up Mr. and Mrs. Whistle, Sister Frances, and Father Stonear. The Whistles insisted that the priest be brought along "just in case." The long black Cadillac traveled quickly down the dirt path along the creek. Once again it was as if the driver was very familiar with the route.

* * *

Sister Mad Marie started to lose steam after she crossed the bridge so Homer grabbed one arm and Harley grabbed the other. The nun's feet did not touch ground until they were at the entrance to the cave.

"They're in there," Harley said dejectedly.

"Look-a-here, this rope must have been on Sweetheart. We all know where he probably took off to," Rhoda Lee explained.

"Poor Fredereek. Hees sveetheart has left him? And hees sveetheart is a he?" asked the baffled nun.

"Sweetheart is a goat, Sister," Eloise said.

"Ve musn't be harsh with the girl or boy or vatever. Eet doesn't matter how she may look... or he may look... or vatever." The nun wiped sweat from her brow. This was all much more complicated than she had realized.

"I'll go after Sweetheart. You can come with me, Sister Madeline. There is somebody I want you to meet. She'll give us a nice cold drink." Eloise took the nun by the arm.

"A drink vould be verrry nice I should think." Eloise guided Sister Madeline to Willa's cabin.

"Now what?" asked Homer.

"We're goin' in." Harley started for the cave entrance clutching the stone around his neck with one hand.

* * *

The spiked heels on Lila Jean's shoes were not the best thing to wear on an old swinging bridge. With every other step she took, the heels would wedge between the old boards. After stopping six times Sister Frances decided to take control.

"Take off those blasted shoes!" Sister Frances yelled in her teacher voice.

"Yes, Sister," Lila Jean whined.

Using her long black rosary beads, Sister Frances looped them through the shoes and let them dangle by the crucifix. She mumbled something about blasphemy as the group inched their way to the other side.

* * *

Harley led, Homer was next, and Rhoda Lee brought up the rear. They had not gone very far into the cave when Harley stopped abruptly.

"Stop! I smell cucumbers! Back out nice and easy!" Harley's tone of voice scared his partners. Once back outside Harley explained. "My Grandpa takes me berry pickin'. When we are in a patch we have to be careful of copperheads." Rhoda Lee took in a sharp breath. "When we smell cucumbers we know to back out 'cuz there's a snake in the berry canes."

"Now what?" asked Homer, a little shaken up.

"We each need a long sturdy stick to take back in with us. Look for a four ta five footer. We're goin' back in. If we come upon a snake just ease the stick under the snake's belly and guide it away from you. Copperheads is shy, not like rattlers.

Stay calm and just ease the snake outa the way. Rhoda Lee, you stay here and wait for the chief."

"No. We gotta help Elmer. I'll be right behind ya." Rhoda Lee gave Homer a look that was not terribly convincing.

The three went to find suitable sticks. Homer found one longer than Rhoda Lee's and swapped with her.

* * *

When Chief Davis, Shirley, and the two nuns came to the opening of the cave there was no one in sight. They all sat down to catch their breath.

* * *

Lila Jean was trying to convince Sister Frances to give her back her shoes when they arrived on the other side of the bridge. It was a heated confrontation. None of the adults knew exactly where they were supposed to be heading. This led to more arguments. Father Stonear fancied himself a tracker and started the group up the hill in the opposite direction of the cave. Shirley was shaking her head as she turned around and headed straight to the cave.

* * *

The copperheads were coiled up. Their tongues flickered as they smelled the two scared boys on the ledge right above them. They started moving smoothly and silently on the floor of the cave.

"Quit farting! They'll smell you and come right up here!" Freddy was in hysterics.

"I cain't help it! I'm scared!" Elmer whined.

Harley could see the glow of a lantern ahead. He heard Elmer and Freddy. At least they were both alive. As the three came into the room where the Civil War skeletons rested, they could barely see the boys on a small ledge above the floor. As their eyes became more adjusted to the darkness they saw the poisonous snakes. There were four of them slithering right below Elmer and Freddy.

"Stay very calm and quiet," Harley instructed. He held his stick out in front of him as he inched closer to the snakes.

"Don't let them bite me!" Freddy screamed.

The snakes reacted to the noise by moving more quickly.

They were unpredictable.

"Be quiet Freddy or you will git us all bit!" Homer said through clenched teeth.

Rhoda Lee could see the problem. With three sticks and four snakes all going different directions, it was a very dangerous situation.

Harley began to go after the closest snake. He slid his stick under the belly, but the snake did not cooperate. It backed off and hissed. Homer tried next. As he was trying to move one snake a different one slid behind him and started to strike. Rhoda Lee yelped as she deftly caught the snake under the head and flipped it over just in time.

"Good one, Rhoda Lee!" Homer looked pale.

"We've got to let them all calm down. Everybody just freeze and stay very quiet." Harley looked Freddy directly in the eye as he said it.

"Kill them!! You've got sticks! Hit them!" Freddy had really lost it then. The snakes responed by slithering toward him. He looked down and whimpered. A small puddle was forming at his feet.

"We've got to do something before he gits us all killed," Harley whispered to Homer and Rhoda Lee. They put their heads together to think.

After a minute or two, Homer said "That just might work."

Rhoda Lee joined Harley and Homer as they made a line behind the snakes. They swept their sticks along the floor of the cave gently. The snakes slithered away from the sticks. They were finally all herded to the far end.

Rhoda Lee helped Elmer out of the cave as Homer dealt with Freddy. He looked like a limp doll. Harley stood guard over the snakes holding the lantern. When he was sure that everyone was out safely he whispered, "Smart move, soldiers. These snakes will make sure nobody ever bothers you again." He saluted the dead Civil War soldiers.

Shirley was the first to hear Rhoda Lee coming out of the cave with Elmer. She ran to her big sister and hugged her. Then she hugged Elmer. Homer followed close behind with Freddy. He handed over the whimpering boy to Sister Frances.

Chief Davis was about to go in after Harley when the boy appeared. The chief shook Harley's hand. That meant a great deal to Harley Hauk.

Coming down the hill were Eloise, Willa, and Sister Madeline looking all refreshed and munching on lemon squares. They were followed by the cutest baby goat that any of them had ever seen, except maybe Elmer. The goat reminded him of Sweetheart when he was just a kid.

Father Stonear had taken his group on a very roundabout path, but they finally arrived just in time to see everyone oohing and ahhing over the new goat whose name was Elmer, just as Willa had promised. Mr. and Mrs. Whistle smiled proudly.

Sister Frances was trying to comfort Frederick Lactkey. He was not responding well to the nun. Sister Madeline tried to intervene, but that only made matters worse.

Freddy scanned the crowd and saw that two people were obviously missing... his mother and father.

The poor little rich boy started to run. The police chief grabbed him by the arm. "Whoa there boy! You got a heap of explainin' to do."

Harley put his hand over the chief's hand and looked up into his eyes. The police officer nodded and released Freddy.

Carefully taking Freddy's arm, Harley pulled out the red string with the small stone on it from around his neck. He put it gently over Freddy's head. Harley led Freddy away from the crowd whispering softly. Everyone watched in astonishment.

"Holy sh....cow!" said Elmer.

ABOUT THE AUTHOR

Donna Ciocca, a New Hampshire resident, is an educator at both the middle school and university levels. She has long been an authority on children's literature, and has been a frequent presenter and keynote speaker at professional conferences and workshops. She has been the recipient of several awards for her contributions to literacy.

Harley & Homer is Donna's first major book, and she has shared its development with her students along the way, much to their delight.

A native of southeastern Missouri, Donna shares the influence of her upbringing with her readers.

The author is married and has three adult sons and two grandchildren.

She is an avid gardener and creative artist.